# Pereira Maintains

# ANTONIO TABUCCHI

# Pereira Maintains
## A Testimony

*Translated by Patrick Creagh*

A NEW DIRECTIONS PAPERBOOK

This translation is published by arrangement with the Harvill Press, London.

Manufactured in the United States of America

First published by New Directions as *Pereira Declares* in 1996 (clothbound) and 1997 (as New Directions Paperbook 848). First published under the title *Pereira Maintains* in 2017 as New Directions Paperbook 1363 (ISBN 978-0-8112-2617-2).

*Library of Congress Cataloging in-Publication Data*
Tabucchi, Antonio, 1943–2012
[Sostiene Pereira. English]
Pereira declares : a testimony / Antonio Tabucchi : translated by Patrick Creagh.
p. cm.
ISBN 978-0-8112-1319-6
Portugal—History—1910–1974—Fiction. I. Creagh, Patrick. II. Title
PQ4880.A24S6613    1996
853'.914—dc20 95-43565

10 9 8 7 6 5 4 3

New Directions Books are published for James Laughlin
by New Directions Publishing Corporation
80 Eighth Avenue, New York 10011

# ONE

Pereira maintains he met him one summer's day. A fine fresh sunny summer's day and Lisbon was sparkling. It would seem that Pereira was in his office biting his pen, the editor-in-chief was away on holiday while he himself was saddled with getting together the culture page, because the *Lisboa* was now to have a culture page and he had been given the job. But he, Pereira, was meditating on death. On that beauteous summer day, with the sun beaming away and the sea breeze off the Atlantic kissing the treetops, and a city glittering, literally glittering beneath his window, and a sky of such a blue as never was seen, Pereira maintains, and of a clarity almost painful to the eyes, he started to think about death. Why so? Pereira cannot presume to say. Maybe because when he was little his father owned an undertaker's establishment with the gloomy name of Pereira La Dolorosa, maybe because his wife had died of consumption some years before, maybe because he was fat and suffered from heart trouble and high blood pressure and the doctor had told him that if he went on like this he wouldn't last long. But the fact is that Pereira began dwelling on death, he maintains. And by chance, purely by chance, he started leafing through a magazine. It was a literary review, though with a section devoted to philosophy. Possibly an avant-garde review, Pereira is not definite on this point, but with a fair share of Catholic contributors. And Pereira was a Catholic, or at least at that moment he felt himself a Catholic, a good Roman Catholic, though there was one thing he could not bring himself to believe in, and that was the resurrection of the body. Of the soul, yes, of course, for he was certain he had a soul; but all that flesh of his, the fat enveloping his soul, no, that would not rise again and why should it? Pereira asked himself. All the blubber he carted around with him day in day out, and the sweat, and the struggle of climbing the stairs, why should all that rise again? No, Pereira didn't fancy it at all, in another life, for all eternity, so he had no wish to believe in the resurrection of the body. And he began to leaf through the magazine, idly, just because he was bored, he maintains, and came across an article headed: "From a thesis delivered last month at the University of Lisbon we publish this reflection on death. The author is Francesco Monteiro Rossi, who graduated last month from the University of Lisbon with a First in Philosophy. We here give only an excerpt from his essay, since he may well make further contributions to this publication."

Pereira maintains that to begin with he read without paying much attention to the article, which was untitled, but then mechanically turned back and copied out a passage. What came over him? Pereira cannot presume to say. Maybe that Catholic-cum-avant-garde magazine got on his nerves, maybe that day he was fed up with Catholicism and the avant-garde in every shape and form, devout Catholic though he was, or maybe again at that particular moment of the particular summer then glittering over Lisbon, with all that bulk of his flesh weighing him down, he detested the idea of the resurrection of the body. But the fact is he set about copying out the article, possibly so as to throw the magazine away as soon as possible.

He didn't copy all of it, he maintains, only a few lines, which he can document and which read as follows: "The relationship that most profoundly and universally characterizes our sense of being is that of life with death, because the limits imposed on our existence by death are crucial to the understanding and evaluation of life." He then picked up the telephone directory and said to himself: Rossi, Rossi, what an unusual name, there can't be more than one Rossi in the telephone book. He dialed a number, he remembers the number well, he maintains, and heard a voice at the other end say hello. Hello, said Pereira, this is the *Lisboa* speaking. And the voice said: yes? Well, said Pereira, he maintains, the *Lisboa* is a Lisbon newspaper founded a few months ago, I don't know whether you have seen it, we are nonpolitical and independent but we believe in the soul, that is to say we have Roman Catholic tendencies, and I would like to speak to Mr. Monteiro Rossi. At the other end, Pereira maintains, there was a moment's silence, and then the voice said that it was Monteiro Rossi speaking and that he didn't give a great deal of thought to the soul. Pereira in turn was silent for a moment or two, for to him it seemed strange, he maintains, that a person who had penned such profound reflections on death should not give much thought to the soul. He therefore assumed there must be some misunderstanding, and at once his mind flew to that resurrection of the body which was a fixation of his, and he said he had read an article on death by Monteiro Rossi, adding that he too, Pereira, did not believe in the resurrection of the body, if that was what Monteiro Rossi had in mind. In a word, Pereira got flustered, and he was angry, mainly with himself, he maintains, at having gone to all this trouble of calling up a stranger and speaking of delicate and indeed intimate matters such as the soul and the resurrection of the body. Pereira could have cursed himself, he maintains, and at first even thought of hanging up, but then for some reason he summoned the strength to continue and said his name was Pereira, Dr. Pereira, that he edited the culture page of the *Lisboa*, and that admittedly for the time being the *Lisboa* was an evening paper, and therefore not in the same league as other newspapers of the capital, but he was sure it would sooner or later make its mark, and it was true that just now the *Lisboa* devoted most of its space to society news, but in a word they had now decided to publish a culture page to come out on Saturdays, and the editorial staff was not yet complete so he needed an outside contributor to do a regular feature.

Pereira maintains that Monteiro Rossi muttered he would come to the office that very day, adding that the work interested him, that any work interested him, because yes, the fact was he badly needed work, now that he'd finished at university and had to earn his own living, but Pereira had the foresight to say no, not in the office for the moment, perhaps it was best to make an appointment to meet somewhere in town. He said this, he maintains, because he had no wish to invite a stranger to that dismal little room in Rua Rodrigo da Fonseca, with the wheeze of its asthmatic fan and the eternal smell of frying spread abroad by the caretaker, a harridan who cast everyone suspicious looks and did nothing but fry fry fry. Nor did he want a stranger to know that the culture staff of the *Lisboa* consisted solely of himself, Pereira, one man sweating with heat and discomfort in that squalid cubbyhole, and in a word, Pereira maintains, he asked if they could meet in town and he, Monteiro Rossi, said: This evening, in Praça da Alegria, there's an open-air dance with guitars and singing, I've been invited to sing a Neapolitan song, I'm half Italian you know, though I don't speak Neapolitan, but anyway the owner of the café has reserved an outside table for me, there'll be a card on it marked Monteiro Rossi, so what about meeting there? Pereira said yes, then hung up and wiped his brow, he maintains, and just then he had the brilliant idea of publishing a short feature entitled "Anniversaries." He thought he'd start it the very next Saturday, so almost unthinkingly, perhaps because he had Italy in mind, he wrote the title "Two Years Ago Died Luigi Pirandello." Then underneath he wrote the subtitle: "In Lisbon the great dramatist first staged his *Sogno (ma forse no)*."

It was the twenty-fifth of July Nineteen Hundred and Thirty-Eight, and Lisbon was glittering in the azure purity of an Atlantic breeze. Pereira maintains.

# TWO

In the afternoon the weather changed, Pereira maintains. The sea breeze suddenly lulled, in from the Atlantic rolled a dense bank of haze, and the city was soon enveloped in a shroud of heat. Before leaving his office Pereira consulted the thermometer, bought at his own expense and hanging on the back of the door. It showed one hundred degrees. Pereira switched off the fan, he passed the caretaker on the stairs, she said good evening Dr. Pereira, once more he inhaled the stench of frying hovering on the staircase and at last emerged into the open. Directly across the road stood the public market of the neighborhood, with two trucks of the Guarda Nacional Republicana parked outside. Pereira knew that all the markets were in a state of unrest because the day before, in Alentejo, the police had killed a carter who supplied the markets, because he was a Socialist. This explained why the Guarda Nacional were stationed outside the market gates. But the *Lisboa* hadn't had the courage to print the news, or rather the assistant editor hadn't, because the editor-in-chief was on holiday at Buçaco, enjoying the cool air and the waters, and who could be expected to have the courage to print news of that sort, that a Socialist carter had been shot down on his wagon in Alentejo and had drenched all his melons with his blood? No one, because the country was gagged, it had no choice, and meanwhile people were dying and the police had things all their own way. Pereira broke out in sweat, he was thinking of death again. And he thought: this city reeks of death, the whole of Europe reeks of death.

He went along to the Café Orquídea, only a few steps down the road just past the kosher butcher, and sat down at a table inside, where at least there were electric fans. Outside it was quite impossible because of the heat. He ordered a lemonade, went to the washroom to rinse his face and hands, ordered a cigar and an evening paper, and Manuel the waiter brought him the *Lisboa* of all things. He hadn't seen the proofs that day, so he leafed through it as if it were any other paper. The first page announced: "World's Most Luxurious Yacht Sailed Today from New York." Pereira stared at the headline for a long time and then looked at the photograph. It showed a group of people in straw hats and shirtsleeves opening bottles of champagne. Pereira broke out in sweat, he maintains, and his thoughts turned again to the resurrection of the body. If I rise from the dead, he thought, will I be stuck with these people in straw hats? He really imagined himself being stuck with those yacht people in some unspecified harbor in eternity. And eternity appeared to him as an insufferable place shrouded in muggy haze, with people speaking English and proposing toasts and exclaiming: Chin chin! Pereira ordered another lemonade. He wondered whether he should go home and have a cool bath or go and call on his priest friend, Don António of the Church of the Mercês, who had been his confessor some years before when his wife died, and to whom he paid a monthly visit. He thought the best thing was to go and see Don António, perhaps it would do him good.

So he went. Pereira maintains that on that occasion he forgot to pay his bill. He got to his feet in a daze, his thoughts elsewhere, and simply walked out, leaving his newspaper on the table along with his hat, maybe because it was so hot he didn't want to wear it anyway, or else because he was like that, objects didn't mean much to him.

Pereira found Father António a complete wreck, he maintains. He had great bags under his eyes and looked as if he hadn't slept for a week. Pereira asked him what was the matter and Father António said: What, haven't you heard? they've murdered a carter on his own cart in Alentejo, and there are workers on strike, here in the city and all over the country, are you living in another world, and you working on a newspaper? look here, Pereira, for goodness' sake go and find out what's happening around you.

Pereira maintains that he was upset by this brief exchange and the way in which he had been sent packing. He asked himself: Am I living in another world? And he was struck by the odd notion that perhaps he was not alive at all, it was as if he were dead. Ever since his wife's death he had been living as if he were dead. Or rather, he did nothing but think of death, of the resurrection of the body which he didn't believe in and nonsense of that sort, and perhaps his life was merely a remnant and a pretense. And he felt done in, he maintains. He managed to drag himself to the nearest tram stop and board a tram that took him as far as Terreiro do Paço. Through the window he watched Lisbon gliding slowly by, his Lisbon: the Avenida da Liberdade with its fine buildings, then the English-style Praça do Rossio, and at Terreiro do Paço he got out and took another tram up the hill towards the Castle. He left it when it reached the Cathedral because he lived close by, in Rua da Saudade. He made heavy weather of it up the steep ramp to where he lived. There he rang the bell for the caretaker because he couldn't be bothered to hunt for the key to the street door, and she, who was also his daily, came to open it. Dr. Pereira, said she, I've fried you a chop for supper. Pereira thanked her and toiled up the stairs, took the key from under the doormat where he always kept it, and let himself in. In the hallway he paused in front of the bookcase, on which stood a photograph of his wife. He had taken that photo himself, in Nineteen Twenty-Seven, during a trip to Madrid, and looming in the background was the vast bulk of the Escorial. Sorry if I'm a bit late, said Pereira.

Pereira maintains that for some time past he had been in the habit of talking to this photo of his wife. He told it what he had done during the day, confided his thoughts to it, asked it for advice. It seems that I'm living in another world, said Pereira to the photograph, even Father António told me so, the problem is that all I do is think about death, it seems to me that the whole world is dead or on the point of death. And then Pereira thought about the child they hadn't had. He had longed for one, but he couldn't ask so much of that frail suffering woman who spent sleepless nights and long stretches in the sanatorium. And this grieved him. For if he'd had a son, a grown-up son to sit at the table with and talk to, he would not have needed to talk to that picture taken on a trip so long ago he could scarcely remember it. And he said: Well, never mind, which was how he always took leave of his wife's photograph. Then he went into the kitchen, sat down at the table and took the cover off the pan with the fried chop in it. The chop was cold, but he couldn't be bothered to heat it up. He always ate it as it was, as the caretaker had left it for him: cold. He made quick work of it, went to the bathroom, washed under his arms, put on a clean shirt, a black tie, and a dab of the Spanish scent remaining in a flask he had bought in Madrid in Nineteen Twenty-Seven. Then he put on a gray jacket and left the flat to make his way to Praça da Alegria. It was already nine o'clock, Pereira maintains.

# THREE

Pereira maintains that the city seemed entirely in the hands of the police that evening. He ran into them everywhere. He took a taxi as far as Terreiro do Paço and there under the colonnade were truckloads of police armed with carbines. Perhaps they were controlling the strategic points of the city in fear of demonstrations or unruly crowds. He would have liked to walk the rest of the way, the cardiologist had told him he ought to take exercise, but he quailed at the thought of passing right under the noses of those sinister militiamen, so he caught the tram which ran the length of Rua dos Fanqueiros and stopped in Praça da Figuera. Here he alighted and found more police, he maintains. This time he was forced to walk past squads of them, and it made him feel pretty uncomfortable. On his way by he heard an officer say to his men: Just remember boys, there could be a Bolshie round every corner, so keep your eyes peeled.

Pereira looked this way and that, as if the advice had been directed at him, but saw no reason to keep his eyes peeled. Avenida da Liberdade was perfectly tranquil, the ice-cream kiosk was open and there were people at the tables enjoying the cool. He strolled peacefully along the central pavement and at this point, he maintains, he first heard the music. The gentle, melancholy guitar music of Coimbra, and it seemed to him odd, that conjunction of music and armed militiamen. It seemed to be coming from Praça da Alegria, and so it proved to be, because the nearer he got the louder grew the music.

In Praça da Alegria there was no sense of being in a besieged city, Pereira maintains, because he saw no police at all, only a night watchman who appeared to be drunk, dozing on a bench. The whole place was decorated with paper festoons and colored light bulbs, green and yellow, hanging on wires strung from window to window. There were a number of tables out in the open and several couples dancing. Then he noticed a banner stretched between two trees, and written on it in enormous letters: LONG LIVE FRANCISCO FRANCO. And beneath this, in smaller letters: LONG LIVE OUR PORTUGUESE TROOPS IN SPAIN.

Pereira maintains that only then did he realize this was a Salazarist festival, and that was why it had no need to be patrolled by troops. And only then did he notice that a lot of people were wearing the green shirt and the scarf knotted round their necks. He hung back in terror, and several different things flashed into his mind at once. It occurred to him that perhaps Monteiro Rossi was one of them, he thought of the Alentejan carter who had shed his blood all over his melons, he tried to imagine what Father António would have said had he seen him there. He thought of all this and flopped down on the bench where the night watchman was dozing, and let himself drift along with his thoughts. Or rather, he let himself drift with the music, because the music, in spite of all, was a pleasure to him. The players were two little old men, one on the viola and the other on the guitar, and they played the heartrending old melodies of the Coimbra of his youth, when he was a student and thought of life as a long radiant future. In those days he too used to play the viola at student parties, he had a trim figure and was athletic and had the girls falling in love with him. Any number of beautiful girls had been mad about him. But he had fallen for a frail, pallid little thing who wrote poetry and had frequent headaches. Then his thoughts turned to other things in his life, but these Pereira has no wish to mention, because he maintains they belong to him and him alone and have nothing to do with that evening and that festival where he had turned up all unsuspecting. And then, Pereira maintains, at a certain point he saw a tall slim young man in a light-colored shirt get up from a table and station himself between the two musicians. And for some reason his heart stood still, maybe because in that young man he seemed to recognize himself, he seemed to rediscover himself as he was in his Coimbra days, because the young man was in some way like him, not in feature but in the way he moved, and something about the hair too, the way a lock flopped onto his forehead. And the young man started singing an Italian song, *O sole mio*, of which Pereira did not understand the words, but it was a song full of passion and vitality, limpid and beautiful, and the only words he understood were "*o sole mio*" and nothing more, and all the while the young man was singing the sea breeze was rising again from the Atlantic and the evening was cool, and everything seemed to him lovely, his past life of which he declines to speak, and Lisbon, and the vault of the sky above the colored lights, and he felt a great nostalgia, did Pereira, but he declines to say for what. However, Pereira realized that the young man singing was the person he had spoken to on the telephone that afternoon, so when the song was over he got up from the bench, because his curiosity was stronger than his misgivings, and made his way to the table and said to the young man: Mr. Monteiro Rossi, I presume. Monteiro Rossi tried to rise to his feet, bumped against the table, and the tankard of beer in front of him toppled over, soaking his pristine white trousers from top to bottom. I do apologize, mumbled Pereira. No, it was my clumsiness, said the young man, it often happens to me, you must be Dr. Pereira of the *Lisboa*, please take a seat. And he held out his hand.

Pereira maintains that he sat down at the table feeling ill at ease. He thought to himself that this was not the place for him at all, that it was absurd to meet a stranger at this nationalist festival, that Father António would not have approved of his conduct, and that he wished he were already on his way home to talk to his wife's picture and ask its forgiveness. These thoughts nerved him to ask a direct question, simply to start the ball rolling, and without much weighing his words he said to Monteiro Rossi: This is a Salazarist Youth festival, are you a member of the Salazarist Youth?

Monteiro Rossi brushed back his lock of hair and replied: I am a graduate in philosophy, my interests are philosophy and literature, but what has your question got to do with the *Lisboa*? It has this to do with it, replied Pereira, that we are a free and independent newspaper and don't wish to meddle in politics.

Meanwhile the two old musicians had struck up again, and from their melancholy strings they elicited a song in praise of Franco, but at that point Pereira, despite his uneasiness, realized he had let himself in for it and it was his business to take the initiative. And strangely enough he felt up to doing so, felt he had the situation in hand, simply because he was Dr. Pereira of the *Lisboa* and the young man facing him was hanging on his lips. So he said: I read your article on death and found it very interesting. Yes, I did write a thesis on death, replied Monteiro Rossi, but let me say at once that it's not all my own work, the passage they printed in the magazine was copied, I must confess, partly from Feuerbach and partly from a French spiritualist, and not even my own professor tumbled to it, teachers are more ignorant than people realize, you know. Pereira maintains that he thought twice about asking the question he'd been preparing all evening, but eventually he made up his mind, not without first ordering something to drink from the young green-shirted waiter in attendance. Forgive me, he said to Monteiro Rossi, but I never touch alcohol, only lemonade, so I'll have a lemonade. And while sipping his lemonade he asked in a low voice, as if someone might overhear and reprove him for it: But are you, please forgive me but, well, what I want to ask is, are you interested in death?

Monteiro Rossi gave a broad grin, and this, Pereira maintains, disconcerted him. What an idea, Dr. Pereira, exclaimed Monteiro

Rossi heartily, what I'm interested in is life. Then, more quietly: Listen, Dr. Pereira, I've had quite enough of death, two years ago my mother died, she was Portuguese and a teacher and she died suddenly from an aneurysm in the brain, that's a complicated way of saying a burst blood vessel, in short she died of a stroke, and last year my father died, he was Italian, a naval engineer at the Lisbon dockyard, and he left me a little something but I've already run through that, I have a grandmother still alive in Italy but I haven't seen her since I was twelve and I don't fancy going to Italy, the situation there seems even worse than ours, and I'm fed up with death, Dr. Pereira, you must excuse me for being frank with you but in any case why this question?

Pereira took a sip of his lemonade, wiped his lips with the back of his hand and said: Simply because in a newspaper one has to have memorial articles on dead writers or an obituary every time an important writer dies, and an obituary can't be written at the drop of a hat, one has to have it ready beforehand, and I'm looking for someone to write advance obituaries on the great writers of our times, imagine if Mauriac were to die tomorrow, how do you think I'd manage?

Monteiro Rossi ordered another beer, Pereira maintains. Since he'd arrived the young man had drunk at least three and at that point, in Pereira's opinion, he ought to be already rather tight, or at least slightly tipsy. Monteiro Rossi swept back his lock of hair and said: Dr. Pereira, I am a good linguist and I know the work of modern writers; what I love is life, but if you want me to write about death and you pay me for it, as they've paid me this evening to sing a Neapolitan song, then I can do it, for the day after tomorrow I'll write you a funeral oration for García Lorca, what d'you think of Lorca? after all he created the avant-garde in Spain just as here in Portugal Pessoa created our modernist movement, and what's more he was an all-round artist, he was a poet, a musician and a painter too.

Pereira said Lorca didn't seem to him the ideal choice, he maintains, but he could certainly give it a try, as long as he dealt with Lorca tactfully and with due caution, referring exclusively to his personality as an artist and without touching on other aspects which in view of the current situation might pose problems. And then, without batting an eyelid, Monteiro Rossi said: Look here, excuse my mentioning it, I'll do you this article on Lorca but d'you think you could give me something in advance? I'll have to buy some new trousers, these are terribly stained, and tomorrow I'm going out with a girl I knew at university who's on her way here now, she's a good chum of mine and I'm very fond of her, I'd like to take her to the cinema.

# FOUR

The girl who turned up had an Italian straw hat on. She was really beautiful, Pereira maintains, her complexion fresh, her eyes green, her arms shapely. She was wearing a dress with straps crossing at the back that showed off her softly molded shoulders.

This is Marta, said Monteiro Rossi, Marta let me introduce Dr. Pereira of the *Lisboa* who has engaged me this evening, from now on I'm a journalist, so you see I've found a job. And she said: How d'you do, I'm Marta. Then, turning to Monteiro Rossi, she said: Heaven knows why I've come to a do of this sort, but since I'm here why don't you take me for a dance, you numskull, the music's nice and it's a marvelous evening.

Pereira sat on alone at the table, ordered another lemonade and drank it in small sips as he watched the young pair dancing slowly cheek to cheek. Pereira maintains that it made him think once again of his own past life, of the children he had never had, but on this subject he has no wish to make further statements. When the dance ended the young people took their places at the table and Marta said rather casually: You know, I bought the *Lisboa* today, it's a pity it doesn't mention the carter the police have murdered in Alentejo, all it talks about is an American yacht, not a very interesting piece of news in my view. And Pereira, guilt-struck for no good reason, replied: The editor-in-chief is on holiday taking the waters, I am only responsible for the culture page because, you know, from next week on the *Lisboa* is going to have a culture page and I am in charge of it.

Marta took off her hat and laid it on the table. From beneath it cascaded a mass of rich brown hair with reddish lights in it, Pereira maintains. She looked a year or two older than her companion, perhaps twenty-six or twenty-seven, so he asked her: What do you do in life? I write business letters for an import-export firm, replied Marta, I only work in the mornings, so in the afternoons I have time to read, go for walks, and sometimes meet Monteiro Rossi. Pereira maintains he found it odd that she called the young man by his surname, Monteiro Rossi, as if they were no more than colleagues, but he made no comment and changed the subject: I thought perhaps you belonged to the Salazarist Youth, he said, just for something to say. And what about you? countered Marta. Oh, said Pereira, my youth has been over for quite a while, and as for politics, apart from the fact that they don't much interest me I don't like fanatical people, it seems to me that the world is full of fanatics. It's important to distinguish between fanaticism and faith, replied Marta, otherwise we couldn't have ideals, such as that men are free and equal, and even brothers, I'm sorry if I'm really only trotting out the message of the French Revolution, do you believe in the French Revolution? Theoretically yes, answered Pereira, and then regretted having said theoretically, because what he had wanted to say was: Substantially yes. But he had more or less conveyed his meaning. And at that point the two little old men with viola and guitar struck up with a waltz and Marta said: Dr. Pereira, I'd like to dance this waltz with you. Pereira rose to his feet, he maintains, gave her his arm and led her onto the dance floor. And he danced that waltz almost in rapture, as if his paunch and all his fat had vanished by magic. And during the dance he looked up at the sky above the colored lights of Praça da Alegria, and he felt infinitely small and at one with the universe. In some nondescript square somewhere in the universe, he thought, there's a fat elderly man dancing with a young girl and meanwhile the stars are circling, the universe is in motion, and maybe someone is watching us from an everlasting observatory. When they returned to their table: Oh why have I no children? thought Pereira, he maintains. He ordered another lemonade, thinking it would do him good because during the afternoon, with that atrocious heat, he'd had trouble with his insides. And meanwhile Marta chattered on as relaxed as you please, and said: Monteiro Rossi has told me about your schemes for the paper, I think they're good, there must be dozens of writers who ought to be kicking the bucket, luckily that insufferable Rapagnetta who called himself D'Annunzio kicked it a few months ago, but there's also that pious fraud Claudel whom we've had quite enough of, don't you think? and I'm sure your paper, which appears to have Catholic leanings, would willingly give him some space, and then there's that scoundrel Marinetti, a nasty piece of work, who after singing the praises of guns and war has gone over to Mussolini's Blackshirts, it's about time he was on his way too. Pereira maintains that he broke out in a slight sweat and whispered: Young lady, lower your voice, I don't know if you realize exactly what kind of a place we're in. At which Marta put her hat back on and said: Well, I'm fed up with it anyway, it's giving me the jitters, in a minute they'll be striking up military marches, I'd better leave you with Monteiro Rossi, I'm sure you have things to discuss so I'll walk down to the river, I need a breath of fresh air, so goodnight.

Pereira maintains that he felt a sense of relief. He finished his lemonade and was tempted to have another but couldn't make up his mind because he didn't know how much longer Monteiro Rossi wanted to stay on, so he asked: What do you say to another round? Monteiro Rossi accepted and said he had the whole evening free and would like to talk about literature, as he had very few opportunities to do so, he usually discussed philosophy, he only knew people exclusively concerned with philosophy. And at this point Pereira was reminded of an oft-repeated saying of an uncle of his, an unsuccessful writer, so he quoted it. He said: Philosophy appears to concern itself only with the truth, but perhaps expresses only fantasies, while literature appears to concern itself only with fantasies, but perhaps it expresses the truth. Monteiro Rossi grinned and said he thought this defined the two disciplines to a T. So Pereira asked him: What do you think of Bernanos? Monteiro Rossi appeared slightly at a loss at first and asked: The Catholic writer, you mean? Pereira nodded and Monteiro Rossi said gently: You know, Dr. Pereira, as I told you on the telephone I don't give a great deal of thought to death, or Catholicism either for that matter, because my father as I said was a naval engineer, a practical man who believed in progress and technology, and brought me up on those lines, although he was Italian I feel that he brought me up more in the English style, with a pragmatical view of life; I love literature but perhaps our tastes don't coincide, at least as regards certain writers, but I do seriously need work and am willing to write advance obituaries for all the writers you ask for, or rather your paper does. It was then, Pereira maintains, that he felt a sudden surge of pride. He maintains it irked him that this young man should be giving him a lecture on professional ethics, and in a word he found it downright disrespectful. He decided to adopt a haughty tone himself, and said: I don't answer to my editor-in-chief for my decisions on literature, I am the editor of the culture page and I choose the writers who interest me, I have made up my mind to give you the job and also to give you a free hand; I would have liked Bernanos and Mauriac because I admire their work, but at this point I leave the decision up to you to do as you think fit. Pereira maintains that he instantly regretted having committed himself to such an extent, he risked trouble with the editor-in-chief by giving a free hand to this youngster whom he scarcely knew and who had openly admitted having copied his degree thesis. For a moment he felt trapped, he realized he had placed himself in a foolish situation. But luckily Monteiro Rossi resumed the conversation and began to talk about Bernanos, whose work he apparently knew quite well. He said: Bernanos has guts, he isn't afraid to speak about the depths of his soul. At the sound of that word, soul, Pereira took heart again, he maintains, as if raised from a sickbed by some healing balm, and this caused him to ask somewhat fatheadedly: Do you believe in the resurrection of the body? I've never given it a thought, replied Monteiro Rossi, it's not a problem that interests me, I assure you it simply isn't a problem that interests me, but I could come to the office tomorrow, I could even do you an advance obituary of Bernanos but frankly I'd rather write a memorial piece on Lorca. Very well, said Pereira, I am the whole editorial staff and you will find me at number sixty-six Rua Rodrigo da Fonseca, near Rua Alexandre Herculano and just a few steps from the kosher butcher, if you meet the caretaker on the stairs don't take fright, she's a harridan, just tell her you have an appointment with Dr. Pereira and don't get chatting with her, she's probably a police informer.

Pereira maintains that he doesn't know why he said this, perhaps simply because he detested the caretaker and the Salazarist police, but the fact is he saw fit to say it, though it wasn't to set up some phony complicity with this young man whom he had only just met; that wasn't it, but the exact reason Pereira doesn't know, he maintains.

# FIVE

When Pereira got up next morning, he maintains, there ready and waiting for him was a cheese omelet sandwiched between two hunks of bread. It was ten o'clock and his daily, Piedade, came in at eight. She had evidently made it for him to take to the office for lunch, because this woman knew his tastes inside out and Pereira adored cheese omelets. He drank a cup of coffee, had a bath, put on a jacket but decided not to wear a tie. However, he slipped one in his pocket. Before leaving the flat he paused in front of his wife's photograph and told it: I've come across a boy called Monteiro Rossi and have decided to take him on as an outside contributor and get him to do advance obituaries, at first I thought he was very bright but he now seems to me a trifle dim, he'd be about the age of our son if we'd had a son, there's even a slight resemblance to me, he has that lock of hair flopping into his eyes, do you remember when I had a lock of hair flopping into mine? it was in our Coimbra days, well, I don't know what else to tell you, we'll just have to wait and see, he's coming to the office today, he says he'll bring me an obituary, he has a beautiful girlfriend with copper-colored hair, called Marta, she's just a bit too cocksure and talks politics but never mind, we'll see how it goes.

He took the tram to Rua Alexandre Herculano, then trudged laboriously on foot up to Rua Rodrigo da Fonseca. When he reached the door he was drenched with sweat, it was a real scorcher. In the hallway as usual he met the caretaker who said: Good morning Dr. Pereira. Pereira gave her a nod and climbed the stairs. The minute he entered the office he got down to shirtsleeves and switched on the fan. He couldn't decide how to spend the time, it was nearly midday. He contemplated eating his omelet sandwich, but it was still early for that. Then he remembered the "Anniversaries" feature and started to write. "Three years ago died the great poet Fernando Pessoa. By education he was English-speaking, but he chose to write in Portuguese because he maintained that his motherland was the Portuguese language. He left us many beautiful poems scattered in various magazines and one long poem, *Message*, which is the history of Portugal as seen by a great artist who loved his country." He read over what he had written and found it nauseating, yes, nauseating was the word, Pereira maintains. So he threw that page away and wrote: "Fernando Pessoa died three years ago. Very few people, almost no one, even knew he existed. He lived in Portugal as a foreigner and a misfit, perhaps because he was everywhere a misfit. He lived alone, in cheap boardinghouses and rented rooms. He is remembered by his friends, his comrades, those who love poetry."

He reached for his omelet sandwich and took a bite. At that very moment he heard a knock at the door, so he hid the omelet sandwich away in a drawer, wiped his mouth on a sheet of onionskin and said: Come in. It was Monteiro Rossi. Good morning Dr. Pereira, said Monteiro Rossi, I'm sorry I'm a bit early but I've brought you something, in fact last night when I got home I had an inspiration, and anyway I thought there was a chance of something to eat here at the *Lisboa*. Pereira patiently explained that that room was not the *Lisboa* itself but a separate office for the culture page, and that he, Pereira, was the whole office staff, he thought he had already made this clear, it was simply a room with a desk and a fan, because the *Lisboa* was only a minor evening paper. Monteiro Rossi sat himself down and pulled out a sheet of paper folded in four. Pereira took it and read it. Unpublishable, Pereira maintains, a completely unpublishable article. It described the death of Lorca, and began as follows: "Two years ago, in obscure circumstances, we lost the great Spanish poet Federico García Lorca. He was assassinated, and suspicion rests on his political opponents. The whole world is still wondering how such an act of barbarism could have been perpetrated."

Pereira looked up from the page and said: My dear Monteiro Rossi, you tell an excellent yarn but my paper is not the proper place for yarns, in newspapers we have to write things that correspond to the truth or at least resemble the truth, it is not up to you to say how a writer died, for what reasons and in what circumstances, you must simply state that he is dead and then go on to speak of his work, of his novels and poems, because when you write an obituary you are essentially making a critical assessment, a portrait of the man and his work, what you have written is absolutely unusable, Lorca's death is still wrapped in mystery and what if things didn't happen as you say they did?

Monteiro Rossi protested that Pereira had not finished reading the article, that further on it dealt with the work, the figure and stature of Lorca as man and artist. Pereira read doggedly on. Dangerous, he maintains, the article was dangerous. It spoke of the hidden depths of Spain, of the rigidly Catholic Spain which Lorca had made the target of his shafts in *The House of Bernarda Alba*, it told of the "Barraca," the traveling theater which Lorca brought to the people. At which point there was a long panegyric on the Spanish working classes and their longing for culture and drama which Lorca had satisfied. Pereira raised his head from the article, he maintains, smoothed back his hair, turned back his cuffs and said: My dear Monteiro Rossi, permit me to be frank with you, your article is unpublishable, completely unpublishable. I cannot publish it, no newspaper in Portugal could publish it, and no Italian paper either, seeing as how Italy is the land of your ancestors, so there are two possibilities: you are either irresponsible or a troublemaker, and journalism nowadays in Portugal has no place for either irresponsibility or troublemaking, and that's that.

Pereira maintains that as he was saying this he felt a trickle of sweat running down his spine. Why was he sweating? Heaven knows. Pereira is unable to say exactly why. Perhaps because the heat was terrific, no doubt of that, and the fan was too feeble to cool even that poky room. But maybe also because his heart was touched by the sight of that youngster looking at him with an air of amazement and disappointment, who even before he finished speaking had begun to gnaw at his fingernails. So he couldn't bring himself to say: Well too bad, it was a try but it hasn't come off, that will be all, thank you. Instead he sat for a while with folded arms looking at Monteiro Rossi until Monteiro Rossi said: I'll rewrite it, I'll rewrite it by tomorrow. At which Pereira plucked up the courage to say: Oh no, that's enough about Lorca if you please, there are too many things about his life and death that won't do for a paper like the *Lisboa*, I don't know whether you are aware of it, my dear Monteiro Rossi, but at this moment there's a civil war raging in Spain, and the Portuguese authorities think along the same lines as General Francisco Franco and for them Lorca was a traitor, yes, traitor is the very word.

Monteiro Rossi got to his feet as if the word struck the fear of God into him, backed towards the door, stopped, came a step forward and said: But I thought I'd found a job. Pereira did not answer, he felt a trickle of sweat running down his spine. Then what must I do? muttered Monteiro Rossi on a note of entreaty. Pereira got up in turn, he maintains, and went and stood by the fan. He said nothing for a minute or two, waiting for the cool air to dry his shirt. You must write me an obituary of Mauriac, he said, or of Bernanos, whichever you prefer, do I make myself clear? But I worked all night, stammered Monteiro Rossi, I expected to be paid, I'm not asking much after all, just enough for a meal today. Pereira would have liked to remind him that the evening before he had advanced him the money for a new pair of trousers, and clearly he could not spend all day every day giving him money, he wasn't his father. He would have liked to be firm and tough. Instead he said: If your problem is a meal, all right I can treat you to lunch, I haven't eaten yet either and I'm quite hungry, I wouldn't say no to a nice grilled fish or a wiener schnitzel, how about you?

Why did Pereira suggest such a thing? Because he lived alone and that room was a torment to him, because he was genuinely hungry, or because his thoughts were running on the photograph of his wife, or for some other reason? This, he maintains, he cannot presume to say.

# SIX

Be that as it may Pereira invited him to lunch, he maintains, and chose a restaurant in the Praça do Rossio. He thought it would suit them down to the ground because after all they were both intellectuals and that café-restaurant was the great meeting place of writers, the Twenties had been its golden age, the avant-garde magazines were virtually produced at its tables, and in a word anyone who was anyone used to go there and maybe some still did.

They made their way down the Avenida da Liberdade in silence and reached the Praça do Rossio. Pereira chose a table inside, because outside under the awning it was like an oven. He looked about him but saw not a single writer, he maintains. The writers must all be on holiday, he remarked to break the silence, off at the sea perhaps or in the country, there's no one left in town but us. Perhaps they've simply stayed at home, replied Monteiro Rossi, they can't be too keen on going places, not in times like these. Pereira felt a pang of melancholy, he maintains, as he weighed those words. He realized that they were indeed alone, that there was no one about to share their anxieties with, in the restaurant there were only two ladies in little hats and a group of four shady-looking characters in a corner. Pereira chose a table rather on its own, tucked his napkin into his collar as usual, and ordered white wine. I'm feeling like an aperitif, he explained to Monteiro Rossi, I don't drink alcohol as a rule but just now I need an aperitif. Monteiro Rossi ordered draft beer and Pereira asked: Don't you like white wine? I prefer beer, replied Monteiro Rossi, it's cooler and lighter and anyway I don't know one wine from another. That's a pity, said Pereira, if you aim to become a good critic you must refine your tastes, you must cultivate them and learn about wine and food and the world at large. Then he added: And literature. And at that point Monteiro Rossi murmured: I have something to confess to you but I'm too scared. Tell me all the same, said Pereira, I'll pretend I haven't understood. Later, said Monteiro Rossi.

Pereira ordered a grilled bream, he maintains, and Monteiro Rossi asked for gazpacho followed by seafood risotto. The risotto arrived in an enormous terra-cotta terrine and Monteiro Rossi ate enough for three people, he polished it off, Pereira maintains, and it was a simply enormous helping. He then pushed back his lock of hair and said: I wouldn't mind an ice cream or even just a lemon sherbet. Pereira made a mental calculation of how much the meal was going to cost him and concluded that a fair part of his weekly wage would go to that restaurant where he had banked on finding half the writers in Lisbon and instead had found only two old ladies in little hats and four shady characters at a corner table. He started sweating again, untucked the napkin from his collar, ordered a glass of iced mineral water and a coffee, then looked Monteiro Rossi in the eye and said: Now spit out what you wanted to confess before lunch. Pereira maintains that Monteiro Rossi lofted his gaze to the ceiling, then lowered it but avoided his eye, then coughed and blushed like a child and said: I feel a little embarrassed, I'm awfully sorry. There's nothing in the world to be ashamed of, said Pereira, provided you haven't stolen anything or dishonored your father and mother. Monteiro Rossi pressed his table napkin to his lips as if he hoped the words wouldn't come out, pushed back the lock of hair from his forehead and said: I don't know how to put it, I know you demand professionalism and that I should use my reason, but the fact is that I preferred to follow other criteria. Explain yourself more clearly, urged Pereira. Well, Monteiro Rossi hemmed and hawed, well, the fact is the heart has its reasons that the reason knows nothing about, and I obeyed the reasons of the heart, perhaps I shouldn't have, perhaps I didn't even want to, but I couldn't help myself, I swear to you that I would have been quite capable of writing an obituary of Lorca by the light of reason alone, but I couldn't help myself. He wiped his mouth with the napkin again and added: What's more I'm in love with Marta. What's that got to do with it? objected Pereira. I don't know, replied Monteiro Rossi, perhaps nothing, but it's reasons of the heart again, don't you think? it's a problem too in its way. The problem is that you oughtn't to get involved with problems bigger than you are, Pereira wanted to say. The problem is that the whole world is a problem and it certainly won't be solved by you or me, Pereira wanted to say. The problem is that you're young, too young, you could easily be my son, Pereira wanted to say, but I don't approve of your making me a father to you, I'm not here to sort out your conflicts. The problem is that between us there must be a correct professional relationship, Pereira wanted to say, and you must learn to write properly, because otherwise, if you're going to base your writing on the reasons of the heart, you'll run up against some awfully big obstacles I can assure you.

But he said nothing of all this. He lit a cigar, wiped the beads of sweat from his forehead, undid the top button of his shirt and said: Yes, the reasons of the heart are the ones that matter most, we must always follow the reasons of the heart, it doesn't say this in the Ten Commandments, it's me saying it, all the same you must keep your eyes open, the heart is all very well, I agree, but keep your eyes open, my dear Monteiro Rossi, and that brings our little luncheon to a close, don't telephone me for the next two or three days, I want to leave you plenty of time to think things over and write something good, and when I say good I mean good, you can call me at the office next Saturday, about midday.

Pereira got up and held out his hand and said: Until then. Why had he said all that when he wanted to say quite the opposite, when he ought to have told him off and perhaps even sacked him? Pereira cannot presume to say. Perhaps because the restaurant was so empty, because he hadn't seen a single writer, because he felt lonely there in town and needed a comforter and a friend? Maybe for these reasons and for others again which he is unable to explain. It's hard to know for sure, when one is dealing with the reasons of the heart, Pereira maintains.

# SEVEN

Arriving at the office on the following Friday, with a package containing his omelet sandwich, Pereira maintains he saw an envelope peeping out of the *Lisboa* mailbox. He fished it out and put it in his pocket. On the first-floor landing he met the caretaker who said: Good morning Dr. Pereira, there's a letter for you, it's an express delivery, the postman brought it at nine o'clock and I had to sign for it. Pereira muttered a thank you between his teeth and went on up the stairs. I took the responsibility on myself, continued the caretaker, but I don't want any trouble, seeing that the sender's name isn't on it. Pereira descended three steps, he maintains, and looked her straight in the face. Look here Celeste, said Pereira, you are the caretaker and that's all well and good, you are paid to be caretaker and receive your wages from the tenants of this building, and one of these tenants is my newspaper, but you have the bad habit of poking your nose into matters that are none of your business, so next time an express letter arrives for me kindly don't sign for it, don't even look at it, but ask the postman to come back later and deliver it to me personally. The caretaker was sweeping the landing, and now leaned her broom against the wall and put her hands on her hips. Dr. Pereira, said she, you think you can address me in that tone because I'm just a humble caretaker, but let me tell you I have friends in high places, people who can protect me from your bad manners. So I imagine, indeed I'm sure of it, Pereira maintains he replied, that's precisely what I object to, and now good day to you.

By the time he opened the office door Pereira was bathed in sweat and felt weak at the knees. He switched on the fan and sat down at his desk. He dumped his omelet sandwich on a sheet of typing paper and took the letter from his pocket. The envelope was addressed to Dr. Pereira, *Lisboa*, Rua Rodrigo da Fonseca 66, Lisbon. The handwriting was stylish and in blue ink. Pereira placed the letter beside the omelet sandwich and lit a cigar. The cardiologist had forbidden him to smoke, but just now he really needed a couple of puffs, then perhaps he'd stub it out. He thought he would open the letter later, because his first task was to prepare the culture page for tomorrow. He considered revising the article he had written on Pessoa for the "Anniversaries" column, but then decided it was all right as it was. So he began to read over the Maupassant story he had translated, in case there were any corrections to be made. He found none. The story read perfectly and Pereira gave himself a pat on the back. It really perked him up a bit, he maintains. Then from his jacket pocket he took a portrait of Maupassant he had come across in a magazine in the City Library. It was a pencil drawing by an unknown French artist, which showed Maupassant wearing an air of desperation, with beard unkempt and eyes staring into space, and Pereira felt it would suit the story perfectly. After all it was a tale of love and death, it cried out for a portrait with intimations of tragedy. Now what he needed was an insert to appear in bold in the center of the article, with the basic biographical facts about Maupassant. Pereira opened the Larousse he kept on his desk and began to copy. He wrote: "Guy de Maupassant, 1850–1893. In common with his brother Hervé he inherited from his father a disease of venereal origin, which led him to madness and an early death. At the age of twenty he fought in the Franco-Prussian War, and thereafter worked at the Ministry of the Navy. A writer of great talent and satirical vision, in his tales he describes the shortcomings and cowardice of a certain stratum of French society. He also wrote very successful novels such as *Bel-Ami* and the fantasy novel *Le Horla*. Struck down by insanity he was admitted to Dr. Blanche's clinic, where he died penniless and derelict."

He took three or four mouthfuls of his omelet sandwich. The rest he threw into the wastepaper basket because he didn't feel hungry, it was too hot, he maintains. Then he opened the letter. It was an article typed on onionskin, and the title read: *Death of Filippo Tommaso Marinetti*. Pereira felt his heart sink because without looking at the next page he knew the writer was Monteiro Rossi and realized at once that the article was no use to him, that it was an unusable article, he could have gone with an obituary for Bernanos or Mauriac, who probably believed in the resurrection of the body, but this was an obituary for Filippo Tommaso Marinetti who believed in war, and Pereira set himself to read it. Truly it was an article to dump straight in the trash, but Pereira did not dump it, God knows why he kept it but he did, and for this reason he is able to produce it as evidence. It began as follows: "With Marinetti dies a man of violence, for violence was his muse. He began his career in 1909 with the publication of a *Futurist Manifesto* in a Paris newspaper, a manifesto in which he idealized war and violence. An enemy of democracy, bellicose and militaristic, he went on to sing the praises of war in a long eccentric poem entitled *Zang Tumb Tumb*, an onomatopoeic description of the Italian colonialist wars in Africa. His colonialist beliefs also led him to acclaim the Italian invasion of Libya. Among his writings is another nauseating manifesto: *War: the World's Only Hygiene*. His photographs show a man striking arrogant poses, with curled mustaches and an academician's cloak covered with medals. The Italian Fascists conferred a great many on him because Marinetti was among their most ardent supporters. With him dies a truly ugly customer, a warmonger ..."

Pereira gave up on the typed section and turned to the letter, for the article was accompanied by a handwritten letter. It read:

"Dear Dr. Pereira, I have followed the reasons of the heart, but it's not my fault. In any case you told me yourself that the reasons of the heart are the most important. I don't know if this is a publishable obituary, and who knows, Marinetti may live for another twenty years. Anyway, if you could let me have something in the way of cash I would be grateful. I can't come to the office at the moment for motives I won't explain now. If you would care to send me a small sum at your discretion, perhaps you could put it in an envelope and address it to me at Box 202, Central Post Office, Lisbon. I'll be giving you a call soon. With best wishes, Yours, Monteiro Rossi."

Pereira placed the obituary and the letter in a file on which he wrote: "Obituaries." Then he numbered the pages of the Maupassant story, gathered up his papers from the desk, put on his jacket and went to deliver the material to the printer's. He was sweating, he felt uneasy, and he hoped not to meet the caretaker on the way out, he maintains.

# EIGHT

That Saturday morning, on the dot of midday, Pereira maintains, the telephone rang. Pereira had not brought his omelet sandwich to the office that day, partly because he was trying to skip a meal every now and again as the cardiologist had advised him, and partly because even if he failed to stave off the pangs of hunger he could always get an omelet at the Café Orquídea.

Good morning Dr. Pereira, said the voice of Monteiro Rossi, this is Monteiro Rossi speaking. I was expecting a call from you, said Pereira, where are you? I am out of town, said Monteiro Rossi. Excuse me, insisted Pereira, but out of town where? Out of town, replied Monteiro Rossi. Pereira maintains he was slightly nettled by such a stiff, uninformative response. From Monteiro Rossi he would have liked more cordiality, even gratitude, but he restrained his vexation and said: I have sent a sum of money to your post office box. Thank you, said Monteiro Rossi, I'll go and pick it up. And he volunteered nothing more. So Pereira asked him: When do you intend to call in at the office? perhaps it would be a good thing to have a tête-à-tête. I've no idea when I'll be able to call on you, replied Monteiro Rossi, to tell the truth I was just writing a note to set up a meeting somewhere, if possible not in the office. It was then that Pereira realized something was up, he maintains, and lowering his voice, as if someone else might be listening in, he asked: Are you in trouble? Monteiro Rossi did not answer and Pereira thought he hadn't heard. Are you in trouble? repeated Pereira. In a way, yes, said the voice of Monteiro Rossi, but it's not something to talk about over the telephone, I'll write you a note to set up a meeting for the middle of next week, the fact is I need you, Dr. Pereira, I need your help, but I'll tell you about it when I see you, and now you must excuse me, I'm calling from somewhere very inconvenient and I have to hang up, forgive me, Dr. Pereira, we'll talk about it when we meet, good-bye for now.

The telephone went click and Pereira hung up in turn. He felt apprehensive, he maintains. He considered what was best to do and made his decisions. First of all he would have a lemonade at the Café Orquídea and stay on there for an omelet. Then, in the afternoon, he would take a train to Coimbra and find his way from there to the baths at Buçaco. He would be sure to meet his editor-in-chief, that was inevitable, and Pereira had no wish to get into conversation with him, but he had a good excuse for not spending any time with him because his friend Silva was also at the spa for his holidays and had often invited him to join him there. Silva was an old college friend at Coimbra now teaching literature at the university, a cultured and sensible man, a levelheaded bachelor, it would be a pleasure to spend two or three days in his company. And in addition he would drink the health-giving waters of the spa, stroll in the gardens and perhaps take a few inhalations, because his breathing was terribly labored, he was often forced to breathe through his mouth, especially when climbing stairs.

He pinned a note to the door: "Back midweek, Pereira." Luckily he did not meet the caretaker and this was some comfort to him. He went out into the blinding midday light and made for the Café Orquídea. As he passed the kosher butcher he noticed a small gathering outside it, so he stopped. He saw that the window was smashed and the shop front covered with scrawls which the butcher was busy covering with white paint. He edged his way through the crowd and went up to the butcher, whom he knew well, young Mayer, he had also known his father well, old Mayer, with whom he had many a time partaken of a lemonade at one of the cafés down by the river. Then old Mayer had died and left the shop to his son David, a hulking youngster with quite a paunch in spite of his youth and a jovial air about him. David, asked Pereira, what's happened here? You can see for yourself, replied David as he wiped his paint-stained hands on his butcher's apron, we live in a world of hooligans, it was the hooligans. Have you called the police? asked Pereira. You must be joking, replied David, you must be joking. And he went on covering the scrawlings with white paint. Pereira walked on to the Café Orquídea and took a seat inside, next to the fan. He ordered a lemonade and took off his jacket. Have you heard what's going on, Dr. Pereira? asked Manuel. Pereira's eyes widened and he asked: The kosher butcher? Kosher butcher my foot, Manuel flung back over his shoulder, that's the least of it.

Pereira ordered an omelet *aux fines herbes* and lingered over it. The *Lisboa* came out at five o'clock and he wouldn't see it because he'd be on the train to Coimbra by then. Perhaps he could send for a morning paper, but he doubted if the Portuguese papers reported the event the waiter was referring to. Rumors simply spread, news traveled by word of mouth, all you could do was ask around in the cafés, listen to gossip, it was the only way of keeping in touch with things, other than buying some foreign paper from the newsagent in Rua do Ouro, but the foreign papers, if they arrived at all, were three or four days old, so it was useless to go hunting for a foreign paper, the best thing was to ask. But Pereira had no wish to ask anyone anything, he simply wanted to get away to the spa, enjoy a day or two of peace and quiet, talk to his friend Professor Silva and not think about all the evil in the world. He ordered another lemonade, asked for his bill, left the café and went to the central post office where he sent two telegrams, one to the hotel at the spa to book a room and the other to his friend Silva: "ARRIVE COIMBRA BY EVENING TRAIN STOP IF YOU CAN MEET ME WITH CAR WOULD BE GRATEFUL STOP AFFECTIONATELY PEREIRA."

Then he went home to pack a suitcase. He thought he would leave buying his ticket until he got to the station, he had all the time in the world, he maintains.

# NINE

When Pereira's train drew in to Coimbra a magnificent sunset was outspread over the city, he maintains. He looked around but saw no sign of his friend Silva on the platform. He supposed the telegram had not arrived or else Silva had left the spa. But on reaching the ticket hall he saw his friend seated on a bench smoking a cigarette. He was delighted and hurried to meet him. He hadn't seen him for quite a while. Silva gave him a hug and took his suitcase. They left the station and walked to the car. Silva had a black Chevrolet with shining chrome, roomy and comfortable.

The road to the spa led through a countryside of lush green hills and was just one bend after another. Pereira wound the window down, he was beginning to feel a little queasy and the fresh air did him good, he maintains. They talked very little during the journey. How are you getting along? asked Silva. So so, replied Pereira. Still living alone? asked Silva. Yes, alone, replied Pereira. I think it's bad for you, said Silva, you ought to find a woman who'd keep you company and cheer your life up a bit, I realize you're still very attached to the memory of your wife, but you can't spend the rest of your life nurturing memories. I'm old, replied Pereira, I'm fat and I've got heart trouble. You're not old at all, said Silva, you're the same age as I am, and after all you could go on a diet, treat yourself to a holiday, take more care of your health. Humph, replied Pereira.

Pereira maintains that the hotel at the spa was a wonder, a shining white mansion set amid spacious gardens. He went up to his room and changed. He donned a light-colored suit and a black tie.

Silva was waiting for him in the lobby sipping an aperitif. Pereira asked if he had seen his editor-in-chief. Silva answered with a wink. He dines every evening with a middle-aged blonde, he replied, she's a guest in the hotel, he appears to have found himself some company. Just as well, said Pereira, it'll let me off having to discuss business.

They entered the restaurant, a nineteenth-century chamber with a ceiling festooned with painted flowers. The editor-in-chief was dining at a center table in the company of a lady in an evening gown. When he looked up and saw Pereira an expression of complete incredulity spread over his face and he beckoned to him. Pereira crossed the room towards him while Silva made his way to another table. Good evening Dr. Pereira, said the editor-in-chief, it comes as a surprise to see you here, have you left the office to its own devices? The culture page came out today, said Pereira, I don't know whether you've seen it yet, possibly the paper hasn't reached Coimbra, there's a Maupassant story and a feature called "Anniversaries" which I've started on my own initiative, and in any case I'm only staying here a few days, on Wednesday I will be back in Lisbon to get the culture page together for next Saturday. My apologies dear lady, said the editor-in-chief addressing his companion, allow me to introduce Dr. Pereira, a member of my staff. Then he added: Senhora Maria do Vale Santares. Pereira inclined his head briefly. There's something I wanted to tell you sir, he said, provided you have no objection, I have decided to engage an assistant to give me a hand purely with advance obituaries of great writers who might die at any moment. Dr. Pereira! exclaimed the editor-in-chief, here I am dining with a gracious, sensitive lady with whom I am conversing about *choses amusantes*, and you come and interrupt us with talk about people who might die at any moment, it seems to me rather less than tactful on your part. I'm very sorry sir, Pereira maintains he said, I didn't intend to talk shop, but on the culture page one needs to foresee the death of great artists, and if one of them dies unexpectedly it's a real problem to compose an obituary overnight, and what's more you'll remember that three years ago when T. E. Lawrence died not a single Portuguese paper got anything out on time, they all came out with their obituaries a week late, and if we want to be an up-to-date paper we must keep abreast of things. The editor-in-chief slowly chewed his way through a mouthful of something and said: Very well, very well, Dr. Pereira, after all I did give you a free hand as regards the culture page, I only want to know whether this assistant is going to cost us much and whether he is a trustworthy person. Oh as far as that's concerned, replied Pereira, he strikes me as an undemanding person, he's a modest young man, and what's more he graduated from Lisbon University with a thesis on death, so he knows about death. The editor-in-chief raised a hand to cut him short, took a sip of wine and said: Come now, Dr. Pereira, stop talking about death if you don't mind or you will ruin our dinner, as for the culture page you may do as you see fit, I have confidence in you, you were a reporter for thirty years after all, and now good evening and enjoy your meal.

Pereira moved over to his table and took a seat opposite his friend. Silva asked if he would like a glass of white wine but he shook his head. He called the waiter and ordered a lemonade. Wine isn't good for me, he explained, the cardiologist told me so. Silva ordered trout with almonds and Pereira ordered a fillet steak *à la Stroganoff* with a poached egg on top. They started eating in silence, then after a while Pereira asked Silva what he thought about all this. All this what? asked Silva. What's going on in Europe, said Pereira. Oh don't bother your head, replied Silva, we're not in Europe here, we're in Portugal. Pereira maintains he couldn't let the matter rest: Yes, but you read the papers and listen to the wireless, he insisted, you know what's going on in

Germany and Italy, they're fanatics, they're out to put the world to fire and sword. Don't bother your head, replied Silva, they're miles away. True enough, said Pereira, but Spain isn't miles away, it's right next door, and you know what's going on in Spain, it's a bloodbath, despite the fact that there was a legally elected government, it's all the fault of one bigot of a general. Even Spain is miles away, said Silva, we're in Portugal here. That may be so, said Pereira, but even here things aren't too rosy, the police have things all their own way, they're killing people, they ransack people's houses, there's censorship, I tell you this is an authoritarian state, the people count for nothing, public opinion counts for nothing. Silva gave him a steady look and laid down his fork. Listen to me Pereira, said Silva, do you still believe in public opinion? well let me tell you public opinion is a gimmick thought up by the English and Americans, it's them who are shitting us up with this public opinion rot, if you'll excuse my language, we've never had their political system, we don't have their traditions, we don't even know what trade unions are, we're a southern people, Pereira, and we obey whoever shouts the loudest and gives the orders. We're not a southern people, objected Pereira, we have Celtic blood in us. But we live in the South, said Silva, the climate here doesn't encourage us to have political opinions, *laissez-faire, laissez-passer*, that's the way we're made, and now listen to me and I'll tell you something else, I teach literature and I know a thing or two about literature, I'm compiling a critical edition of our troubadours, the *Cantigas de amigo*, surely you remember them from university, in any case the young men went off to the wars and the women stayed at home and wept, and the troubadours recorded their laments, because everyone had to do what the king commanded, don't you see? the big chief gave the orders, we've always needed a big chief, and we still need one today. But I'm a journalist, said Pereira. So what? said Silva. So, said Pereira, I must be free to keep people properly informed. I don't see the connection, said Silva, you don't write political stuff, your business is the culture page. Now it was Pereira's turn to lay down his fork and prop his elbows on the table. Listen to me old man, said he, just imagine if Marinetti died tomorrow, you've heard of Marinetti? Vaguely, said Silva. Well then, said Pereira, Marinetti's a swine, he started his career by singing the praises of war, he's set himself up as a champion of bloodshed, he's a terrorist, he hailed Mussolini's march on Rome, Marinetti is a swine and it's my duty to say so. Then go and live in England, said Silva, there you can say whatever you like, you'll have loads of readers. Pereira finished his last mouthful of steak. I'm going to bed, he said, England's too far away. Don't you want any dessert? asked Silva, I could go for a piece of cake. Sweet things are bad for me, said Pereira, the cardiologist told me so, and what's more I'm tired from the journey, but thank you for coming to fetch me from the station, good night, see you tomorrow.

Pereira got up and went off without another word. He was worn to a shred, he maintains.

# TEN

Next morning Pereira woke at six. He had a cup of black coffee, though he had to press for it, he maintains, because room service only started at seven. Then he went for a walk in the gardens. The baths also opened at seven, and at seven on the dot Pereira was at the gates. Silva wasn't there, the editor-in-chief wasn't there, there was practically no one at all and Pereira maintains it was a great relief. He started by drinking two glasses of water tasting of rotten eggs, after which he felt slightly sick and his insides began to churn around. He would have appreciated a nice cool lemonade, because despite the early hour it was already getting hot, but he thought he shouldn't mix lemonade and sulfur water. Then he went to the bathhouses where they made him strip and put on a white bathrobe. Mud bath or inhalations? asked the receptionist. Both, replied Pereira. He was ushered into a room containing a marble bathtub full of brownish liquid. Pereira removed his bathrobe and climbed in. The mud was lukewarm and gave him a feeling of well-being. At a certain point an attendant came in and asked him where he needed massage. Pereira told him he didn't want massage at all, only the bath, and would prefer to be left in peace. When he got out of the tub he had a cool shower, donned the bathrobe again and went next door where there were jets of steam for inhalation. In front of these jets lots of people were already seated, their elbows propped on a marble shelf, breathing in blasts of hot air. Pereira found a free spot and sat down. He breathed deeply for several minutes, and lost himself in his thoughts. These turned to Monteiro Rossi, and for some reason also to his wife's photograph. It was nearly two days since he had talked to his wife's photograph and Pereira maintains he regretted not bringing it with him. He got to his feet, went back to the changing rooms, got dressed, put on his black tie, then left the baths and returned to the hotel. In the restaurant he spied his friend Silva chowing down on croissants and café au lait. Fortunately the editor-in-chief was not to be seen. Pereira went up to Silva, bade him good morning, told him he had taken the waters and continued: There's a train for Lisbon at about midday, I'd be grateful for a lift to the station, if you can't manage it I'll take the hotel taxi. What, off already? exclaimed Silva, I was hoping to spend a couple of days with you. You must forgive me, but I have to be back in town this evening, lied Pereira, I have an important article to write tomorrow, and anyway, you know, I don't like the idea of leaving the office in the hands of the care-taker, so I'd really rather get back. It's up to you, replied Silva, I'll certainly give you a lift.

During the drive they said nothing at all. Pereira maintains that Silva seemed to be in a huff, but he himself did nothing to make things easier. Never mind, he thought, never mind. They reached the station at eleven-fifteen and the train was waiting at the plat-form. Pereira climbed aboard and waved good-bye through the window. Silva gave him a hearty wave in return and went his way.

Pereira took a seat in a compartment where a woman reading a book was already seated. She was handsome, blonde and chic, with a wooden leg. As she was in a window seat Pereira took a place by the corridor so as not to disturb her. He noticed, however, that she was reading a book by Thomas Mann, and in German at that. This aroused his curiosity, but for the moment he said nothing except good morning Senhora. The train pulled out at eleven-thirty and a few minutes later the waiter came round to take reservations for the dining car. Pereira reserved a place because he felt that his stom-ach was a little upset, he maintains, and needed something to settle it. It wasn't a long journey, to be sure, but they would reach Lisbon rather late for lunch, and he had no wish to go searching around for somewhere to eat when he got there, not in that heat.

The lady with the wooden leg also reserved a place in the dining car. Pereira noticed that she spoke good Portuguese but with a slight foreign accent. This, he maintains, redoubled his curiosity and steeled him to make a suggestion. Senhora, said he, please forgive me, I have no wish to be intrusive, but seeing that we are traveling companions and have both made a reservation I suggest we share a table, we can enjoy a little conversation and perhaps feel less lonely, eating alone is so gloomy, especially on a train, allow me to introduce myself, I am Dr. Pereira, editor of the culture page of the *Lisboa*, an evening paper published in Lisbon. The lady with the wooden leg gave him a broad smile and held out her hand. Very glad to meet you, said she, my name is Ingeborg Delgado, I am German but of Portuguese ancestry, I have come to Portugal to rediscover my roots.

The waiter came by ringing the bell for lunch. Pereira got up and stood aside for Senhora Delgado. He did not presume to offer her his arm, he maintains, because he thought this might be mortifying to a lady with a wooden leg. But Senhora Delgado moved pretty smartly despite her artificial limb, and led the way along the corridor. The dining car was close to their compartment so luckily their walk was a short one. They chose a table on the left-hand side of the train. Pereira tucked his napkin into the collar of his shirt and immediately felt embarrassed about it. Forgive me, he said, but when I eat I always seem to mess up my shirt, my daily says I'm worse than a child, I hope you don't think I'm too provincial. Meanwhile outside the train window flowed the gentle landscape of central Portugal, with its green pine-covered hills and dazzling white villages, and now and then the black dot of a peasant working in the vineyards. Do you like Portugal? asked Pereira. Yes, I do, replied Senhora Delgado, but I doubt I'll be staying here long, I have visited my relatives in Coimbra, I have rediscovered my roots, but this is not a country for me or for people of my race, I am awaiting a visa from the American Embassy and soon, I hope, I will be leaving for the United States. Pereira thought he caught her meaning so he asked: Are you Jewish? Yes, I am Jewish, confirmed Senhora Delgado, and Europe in these times is not a suitable place for people of my race, especially Germany, but even here we are not very popular, I can tell it from the newspapers, perhaps the paper you work for is an exception, even if it seems so Roman Catholic in its views, too much so for non-Catholics like myself. But this is a Catholic country, replied Pereira, and I ought to tell you that I'm a Catholic myself, even if in my own way, unfortunately we did have the Inquisition and that doesn't do us much credit, but I, for example, don't believe in the resurrection of the body, I don't know if that means anything to you? I've no idea what it means, said Senhora Delgado, but I'm fairly sure it's none of my business. I noticed you were reading a book by Thomas Mann, said Pereira, he's a writer I very much admire. He too is not happy about what's going on in Germany, said Senhora Delgado, I don't think he's happy about it at all. Maybe I'm not happy about what's going on in Portugal, admitted Pereira. Senhora Delgado took a sip of mineral water and said: Then do something about it. Such as what? asked Pereira. Well, said Senhora Delgado, you're an intellectual, tell people what's going on in Europe, tell them your own honest opinion, just get on and do something. There were many things he would have liked to say, Pereira maintains. He would have liked to tell her that his editor-in-chief was a bigwig in the regime, and worse still there was the regime itself, with its police and its censorship, and that everyone in Portugal was gagged, and that no one in short could express his own honest opinion, and that he personally spent his days in a wretched little hole in Rua Rodrigo da Fonseca in the company of an asthmatic fan and under the eye of a caretaker who was probably a police informer. But Pereira said none of this, all he said was: I'll do my best Senhora Delgado, but it isn't easy to do one's best in a country like this for a person like me, you know, I'm not Thomas Mann, I'm only the obscure editor of the culture page of a second-rate evening paper, I write up the anniversaries of famous authors and translate nineteenth-century French stories, and more than that I cannot do. I understand, replied Senhora Delgado, but surely there's nothing one can't do if one cares enough. Pereira looked out of the window and sighed. They were nearing Vila Franca, already within sight of the long snaking course of the Tagus. How beautiful it was, this little land of Portugal, blessed by the sea and its gentle seaborne climate, but it was all so difficult, thought Pereira. Senhora Delgado, he said, we shall soon be reaching Lisbon, we are at Vila Franca, a town of honest workers, of laboring folk, we in this small country also have our opposition, albeit a silent opposition, perhaps because we have no Thomas Mann, but we do what little we can, and now perhaps we'd better return to our compartment and prepare our bags, I'm truly glad to have met you and had this chat with you, allow me to offer you my arm but don't think of it as a gesture of assistance, it is only a gesture of chivalry, because you know here in Portugal we are very chivalrous.

Pereira got up and offered his arm to Senhora Delgado. She accepted it with the trace of a smile and rose with some difficulty from the cramped table. Pereira paid the bill and added something for a tip. He left the dining car with Senhora Delgado on his arm, feeling very gratified and rather troubled, though without knowing why, he maintains.

# ELEVEN

Pereira maintains that on reaching the office the following Tuesday he met the caretaker, who handed him an express letter. Celeste passed it over with a mocking air and said: I gave your instructions to the postman, but he can't come back later because he has to do the round of the whole neighborhood, so he left this express letter with me. Pereira took it, nodded his thanks and looked to see if the sender's name was on the back. Luckily it wasn't so Celeste had got nothing for her pains. However he instantly recognized Monteiro Rossi's blue ink and florid hand. He entered the office and switched on the fan. Then he opened the letter. It read: "Dear Dr. Pereira, unfortunately I am going through a tricky period. I urgently need to talk to you but I'd rather not come to the office. May I hope to see you at eight-thirty on Tuesday evening at the Café Orquídea? I would very much like to have supper with you and tell you my problems. Hopefully yours, Monteiro Rossi."

Pereira maintains that for the "Anniversaries" column he had in mind a short piece on Rilke, who had died in Twenty-Six, so it was just twelve years since his death. Also he'd begun translating a story by Balzac. He had chosen "Honorine," a story about repentance which he intended to publish in three or four installments. Pereira does not know why, but he had a feeling this story about repentance might come into someone's life like a message in a bottle. Because there were so many things to repent of, he maintains, and a story about repentance was certainly called for, and this was the only way he had of sending a message to someone ready and willing to receive it. So he put his Larousse under his arm, switched off the fan and started home.

When his taxi reached the cathedral the heat was appalling. Pereira removed his tie and put it in his pocket. He climbed laboriously up the steep ramp leading to his house, opened the street door and sat down inside on the bottom step. He was panting heavily. He felt in his pocket for the pills the cardiologist had prescribed for his heart and swallowed one dry. He mopped away the sweat, took a moment's rest in the cool dark hallway, then clambered up to his flat. The caretaker Piedade had left no food for him because she was away with her relatives in Setúbal and would only return in September, like every other year. This depressed him not a little. He didn't care for being on his own, completely on his own, with no one to look after him. He passed his wife's photograph and told it: I'll be back in ten minutes. Then he went through to the bedroom, undressed and turned on the bath. The cardiologist had ordered him not to have his baths too freezing cold, but now he really needed a cold one. So he waited until the bath was full and then got in up to his chin. While he was in the water he spent a long time stroking his paunch. Pereira, he told himself, once upon a time your life was a different kettle of fish. He dried himself, put on his pajamas, then went through into the hall, stopped before his wife's photograph and said: This evening I'm seeing Monteiro Rossi, I don't know why I don't give him the sack and tell him to go to hell, he's got problems which he wants to unload on me, I've understood that much, what do you think about it, what should I do? His wife's photograph replied with a faraway smile. Right you are then, said Pereira, I will now go and have a siesta, and after that I'll find out what that young fellow wants. And off he went to lie down.

That afternoon, Pereira maintains, he had a dream. It was beautiful dream about his youth, but he prefers not to relate it, because dreams ought not to be told, he maintains. He will go no farther than to say he was happy, that it was winter and he was on a beach to the north of Coimbra, perhaps at Granja, and that he had with him a person whose identity he does not wish to disclose. Anyway, he awoke in a good mood, put on a short-sleeved shirt, didn't even pocket a tie, though he did take a light cotton jacket, carrying it over his forearm. The evening was hot, though happily there was a bit of a breeze. At first he considered going all the way to the Café Orquídea on foot, but on second thought this seemed folly. However he did walk as far as Terreiro do Paço and the exercise did him good. From there he took a tram to Rua Alexandre Herculano. The Café Orquídea was practically deserted, Monteiro Rossi had not yet arrived because he himself was too early. Pereira sat himself down at a table inside, near the fan, and ordered a lemonade. When the waiter came he asked him: What's the news Manuel? If you don't know, Dr. Pereira, and you a journalist! replied the waiter. I've been away at Buçaco, at the spa, replied Pereira, I haven't seen the papers, and anyway you never learn anything from the papers, the best thing is to find out by word of mouth and that's why I'm asking you, Manuel. Barbarous goings-on, Dr. Pereira, replied the waiter, barbarous goings-on. And he went about his business.

At this point in came Monteiro Rossi. He approached with that sheepish air of his, peering furtively this way and that. Pereira noticed he was wearing a brand-new shirt, blue with a white collar. It flashed upon Pereira that it had been bought with his money, but he had no time to dwell on this fact because Monteiro Rossi spotted him and came on over. They shook hands. Take a seat, said Pereira. Monteiro Rossi took a seat and said nothing. Well now, said Pereira, what would you like to eat? here they only serve omelets *aux fines herbes* and seafood salad. I could really do with a couple of omelets *aux fines herbes*, said Monteiro Rossi, I'm afraid you'll think it's very forward of me but I didn't get any lunch to-day. Pereira ordered three omelets *aux fines herbes* after which he said: Now tell me your problems, seeing that's how you put it in your letter. Monteiro Rossi pushed back his lock of hair and that gesture had a weird effect on Pereira, he maintains. Well, said Monteiro Rossi lowering his voice, I'm in a pickle, Dr. Pereira, and that's the truth of it. The waiter arrived with the omelets and Monteiro Rossi changed the subject. Ah, what sweltering weather we're having, he said. All the while the waiter was serving them they talked about the weather and Pereira told how he had been at the baths at Buçaco, how the climate there was a treat, up there in the hills and with all that greenery in the gardens. Then the waiter left them and Pereira said: Well? Well, I don't know where to begin, said Monteiro Rossi, I'm in a pickle, that's the long and the short if it. Pereira took a forkful of omelet and asked: Is it to do with Marta?

Why did Pereira ask such a question? Because he really thought that Marta could make trouble for this young man, because he had found her too uppity and sure of herself, because he would have liked things to be otherwise, for the pair of them to be in France or England where uppity, brash girls can say whatever they please? This Pereira cannot presume to say, but the fact is he asked: Is it to do with Marta? Partly yes, replied Monteiro Rossi in a low voice, but I can't blame her, she has her own ideas and they're as solid as a rock. Well? queried Pereira. Well, what has happened is that a cousin of mine has arrived, said Monteiro Rossi. That doesn't sound so awful, replied Pereira, we all have cousins. True enough, said Monteiro Rossi almost in a whisper, but my cousin has come from Spain, he's in an international brigade, he's fighting on the republican side, he's here in Portugal to recruit Portuguese volunteers for this international brigade, I can't have him stay with me, he has an Argentine passport which you can see is a fake from a mile off, so I'm at my wits' end where to put him, where to hide him. Pereira felt sweat beginning to trickle down his back, but he kept calm. Well? he asked, going on with his omelet. So what it needs is you, said Monteiro Rossi, it needs you,

Dr. Pereira, to help him out, to find him some unobtrusive place to stay, it needn't be clandestine just as long as it's somewhere, I can't keep him at home because the police may be suspicious on account of Marta, I might even be under surveillance. Well? asked Pereira yet again. Well, no one suspects you, said Monteiro Rossi, he'll be here for several days, just as long as it takes to make contact with the resistance, then he'll go back to Spain, please help me Dr. Pereira, please find him somewhere to stay.

Pereira finished his omelet, beckoned to the waiter and ordered another lemonade. I am astounded by your impudence, he said, I don't know if you realize what you are asking of me, and anyway what am I supposed to find? A room to rent, said Monteiro Rossi, a cheap hotel, somewhere they're not too fussy about documents, you must know places like that, considering all the people you know.

All the people you know! thought Pereira. But what if with all the people he knew he still didn't really know anyone, he knew Father António whom he could scarcely burden with a problem like this, he knew his friend Silva who was away at Coimbra and couldn't be trusted anyway, and there was the caretaker at Rua Rodrigo da Fonseca who was most probably a police spy. But then he was suddenly reminded of a little flophouse in La Graça, up beyond the Castle, where illicit couples used to go and they never asked for anyone's documents. Pereira knew of it because his friend Silva had once asked him to book a room in some such unobtrusive place for him to spend a night with a Lisbon lady who couldn't risk scandal. So he said: I'll see about it tomorrow morning, but don't send or bring your cousin to the office, because of the caretaker, bring him round at eleven o'clock tomorrow morning to my home and then stay around yourself, I may need you, I'll give you the address right away, but no telephone calls if you please.

Why did Pereira say all this? Because he felt sorry for Monteiro Rossi? Because he had been at the spa and had such a disheartening conversation with his friend Silva? Because on the train he had met Senhora Delgado who had told him that he must do something, be it never so little? Pereira has no idea, he maintains. He only knows that clearly he had gotten himself into a fix and needed to talk to someone about it. But this someone was not in the offing so he thought that when he got home he would talk it over with the photograph of his wife. And that, he maintains, is what he did.

# TWELVE

On the dot of eleven, Pereira maintains, his doorbell rang. He'd got up early, had breakfast, and made a jug of lemonade packed with ice, which now stood on the dining room table. Monteiro Rossi came in with a furtive air and a muttered good morning. Pereira, slightly perplexed, closed the door and asked if his cousin wasn't coming after all. Oh yes, he's here, replied Monteiro Rossi, but he doesn't like to burst in just like that, he's sent me on ahead to have a gander. A gander at what? asked Pereira rather huffily, do you think you're playing at cops and robbers, or did you imagine the police were here waiting for you? Oh it isn't that, Dr. Pereira, apologized Monteiro Rossi, it's just that my cousin is all on edge, he's in a difficult position you know, he's here on a delicate mission, he has an Argentine passport and doesn't know which way to turn. You told me all that last night, retorted Pereira, and now please call him in, that's quite enough of this tomfoolery. Monteiro Rossi opened the door and beckoned. Come on in Bruno, he said in Italian, the coast is clear.

And in there came a skinny little shrimp, with hair cut *en brosse*, a yellowish mustache and a blue jacket. Dr. Pereira, said Monteiro Rossi, let me introduce my cousin Bruno Rossi, however as the name on his passport is Bruno Lugones it'd be better to make a point of calling him Lugones. What language can we talk in? asked Pereira, does your cousin speak Portuguese? No, said Monteiro Rossi, but he speaks Spanish.

Pereira seated them at the dining table and helped them to lemonade. This Bruno Rossi said not a word, but darted suspicious glances this way and that. At the distant siren of an ambulance he stiffened and went over to the window Tell him to relax, Pereira advised Monteiro Rossi, we're not in Spain here, there's no civil war on. Bruno Rossi returned to his seat and said: *Perdone la molestia pero estoy aqui por la causa republicana.* Listen here Senhor Lugones, said Pereira in Portuguese, I will speak slowly so that you can understand me, I am not interested either in the republican or in the monarchist cause, I edit the culture page of an evening paper and such things do not fall within my province. I have found you some out-of-the-way accommodation, more than that I cannot do, and you will kindly take care not to come calling on me because I want nothing to do with either you or your cause. This Bruno Rossi turned to his cousin and said in Italian: He isn't at all how you described him, I expected to find a comrade. Pereira caught the meaning and said: I am nobody's comrade, I am a lone wolf and like it, my only comrade is myself, I don't know if I make myself clear Senhor Lugones, that being the name on your passport. Yes, yes, said Monteiro Rossi almost tripping over his tongue, but the fact is that, well, the fact is we need your help and understanding, because we need money. What exactly do you mean? asked Pereira. Well, said Monteiro Rossi, my cousin has no money and if we get to the hotel and they want payment in advance we can't fork out, not for the moment, I'll put things straight afterwards, or rather Marta will, it'll only be a loan.

On hearing this Pereira stood up, he maintains. He apologized, saying: Please excuse me but I need a few moments' thought, all I ask is a couple of minutes. He left the two of them alone at the dining table and went through into the hall. Standing before his wife's photograph he told it: You know, it's not so much this Lugones who worries me, it's Marta, in my opinion she's the one to blame for all this, Marta is Monteiro Rossi's girl, the one with the copper-colored hair, I think I mentioned her to you, well, she's the one who's getting Monteiro Rossi in trouble, and he's allowing himself to be got into trouble because he's in love with her, I ought to drop him a word of warning, don't you think? His wife's photograph smiled its faraway smile and Pereira thought he'd got its message. He returned to the dining room and asked Monteiro Rossi: Why Marta? what's Marta got to do with it? Oh well, babbled Monteiro Rossi blushing slightly, because Marta has a lot of resources behind her, that's all. You listen to me carefully, Monteiro Rossi, said Pereira, I can't help feeling that you're getting into trouble all because of a beautiful girl, but anyway I'm not your father and don't wish to adopt a fatherly air in case you think it patronizing, so there's only one thing I wish to say to you: take care. Yes, yes, said Monteiro Rossi, I am taking care but what about the loan? We'll see to that, replied Pereira, but why should it have to come from me of all people? But Dr. Pereira, said Monteiro Rossi, digging a sheet of paper from his pocket and holding it out to him, I've written this article and I'll write two more next week, I took the liberty of doing an anniversary, I've done D'Annunzio, I've put my heart into it but my reason as well, as you advised me, and I promise you that the next two will be Catholic writers of the kind you're so keen on.

A flush of irritation came over Pereira, he maintains. Now look here, he said, it's not that I want nothing but Catholic writers, but someone who's written a thesis on death might give a little more thought to the writers who have dealt with this subject, who are interested in the soul, in short, and instead you bring me an anniversary article on a downright vitalist like D'Annunzio, who may possibly have been a good poet but who frittered his life away in frivolities, and my newspaper doesn't care for frivolous people, or at least I don't, do I make myself clear? Perfectly, said Monteiro Rossi, I've got the message. Good, said Pereira, then now let's get along to this hotel, I've remembered a cheap hotel in the Graça where they don't make a lot of fuss, I will pay the advance if they ask for it, however I expect at least two more obituaries from you, Monteiro Rossi, this is your two weeks' wages. I should tell you, Dr. Pereira, said Monteiro Rossi, that I did that anniversary article on D'Annunzio because last Saturday I bought the *Lisboa* and saw there's a feature called "Anniversaries," it isn't signed but I imagine you write it yourself, but if you'd like a hand I'd be very willing to give you one, I'd like to work on that sort of feature, there are loads of authors I could write about, and what's more, seeing as how it's printed anonymously there'd be no risk of getting you into trouble. So you are in trouble are you? Pereira maintains he said. Well, a little, as you can see, replied Monteiro Rossi, but if you prefer a pseudonym I've thought one up, what do you think of Roxy? That would do fine, said Pereira. He removed the lemonade jug, placed it in the ice chest, and putting on his jacket: Very well, let's be on our way, he said.

They left the flat. In the little square outside the building a soldier was sleeping stretched out on a bench. Pereira admitted that he was in no fit state to make it up the hill on foot, so they waited for a taxi. The sun was implacable, Pereira maintains, and the wind had dropped. A taxi came cruising past and Pereira hailed it. During the ride not a word was spoken. They alighted beside a granite cross towering over a tiny chapel. Pereira entered the hotel, advising Monteiro Rossi to wait outside but taking his cousin in with him and presenting him to the desk clerk, a little old man with pebble glasses who was dozing behind the counter. I have here an Argentine friend, said Pereira, he is Señor Bruno Lugones, here's his passport, he would like to remain incognito, he is here for sentimental reasons. The old man took off his spectacles and leafed through the register. Someone telephoned this morning to make a reservation, he said, was that you? It was me, confirmed Pereira. We have a double room without bath, said the old man, I don't know if that would do for the gentleman. It will do very well, said Pereira. Cash in advance, said the old man, you know how things are. Pereira took out his wallet and produced a couple of banknotes. I'll pay for three days in advance, he said, and good morning to you. He waved a hand at Bruno Rossi but decided not to shake hands, he didn't want to seem on such intimate terms. I hope you'll be comfortable, he said.

He left the place and crossed the square to where Monteiro Rossi was sitting waiting on the edge of the fountain. Call in at the office tomorrow, he told him, I'll read your article today, we have things to talk about. Well actually I . . . , began Monteiro Rossi. Actually what? asked Pereira. Well you know, said Monteiro Rossi, as things stand I thought it would be better for us to meet in some quiet spot, perhaps at your flat. I agree, said Pereira, but not at my flat, enough of that, let's meet at one o'clock tomorrow at the Café Orquídea, would that suit you? Right you are, replied Monteiro Rossi, the Café Orquídea at one o'clock. Pereira shook hands and said: See you tomorrow. Since it was downhill all the way he thought he'd go home on foot. It was a splendid day and luckily a bracing Atlantic breeze had now sprung up. But he felt in no mood to appreciate the weather. He felt uneasy and would have liked to have a talk with someone, perhaps Father António, but Father António spent all day at the bedsides of his sick parishioners. It occurred to him that he could chat with the photograph of his wife. So taking off his jacket he made his way slowly homeward, he maintains.

# THIRTEEN

Pereira spent that night on the final stages of translating and editing Balzac's "Honorine." It was a hard job, but in his opinion it read pretty fluently, he maintains. He slept for three hours, from six until nine in the morning, then got up, had a cold bath, drank a cup of coffee and went to the office. The caretaker, whom he met on the stairs, gave him a surly look and a curt nod. He muttered a good morning, went on up to his room, sat down at the desk and dialed the number of Dr. Costa, his medical adviser. Hello, hello Dr. Costa, said Pereira, this is Pereira speaking. How are you feeling? inquired Dr. Costa. I'm awfully short of breath, replied Pereira, I can't climb stairs and I think I've put on several pounds, whenever I go for a stroll my heart starts thumping. I'll tell you something, Pereira, said Dr. Costa, I do a weekly consultancy at a thalassotherapeutic clinic at Parede, why don't you spend a few days there? In a clinic? asked Pereira, why? Because the clinic at Parede has really good medical supervision, and what's more they use natural remedies for cardiopathic and rheumatic cases, they give seaweed baths and massages and weight-losing treatment, and they have some first-rate French-trained doctors, it would do you good to have a bit of rest and supervision, Pereira, and the Parede clinic is just the place for you, if you like I can book you a room for tomorrow even, a nice cozy little room with a sea view, a healthy life, seaweed baths, thalassotherapy, and I'll be in to see you at least once, there are a few tubercular patients but they're in a separate wing, there's no danger of infection. Oh don't imagine I'm worried about tuberculosis, replied Pereira, I spent most of my life with a consumptive and the disease never affected me at all, but that isn't the problem, the problem is that they've put me in charge of the Saturday culture page and I can't leave the office. Now then Pereira, said Dr. Costa, get this straight, Parede is half-way between Lisbon and Cascais, it's barely six miles from here, if you want to write your articles at Parede and send them to Lisbon, someone from the clinic comes to town every morning and could deliver them, and in any case your page only comes out once a week so if you prepare a couple of good long articles the page is ready for two Saturdays ahead, and furthermore let me tell you that health is more important than culture. Oh, very well, said Pereira, but two weeks is too long, one week's rest is enough for me. Better than nothing, conceded Dr. Costa. Pereira maintains that he resigned himself to spending a week in the thalassother-apeutic clinic at Parede, and authorized Dr. Costa to book him a room for the following day, but made a point of specifying that he must first notify his editor-in-chief, as a matter of form. He hung up and began by dialing the number of the printer's. He said he had a story of Balzac's ready to set up in either two or three installments, and that the culture page was therefore in hand for several weeks to come. What about the "Anniversaries" column? asked the printer. No anniversaries for the moment, said Pereira, and don't come to fetch the stuff from the office because I won't be here this afternoon, I'll leave it in a sealed envelope at the Café Orquídea, near the kosher butcher. Then he called the exchange and asked the operator to connect him with the spa at Buçaco. He asked to speak to the editor-in-chief of the *Lisboa*. The editor is in the garden taking the sun, said the hotel clerk, I don't know if I ought to disturb him. Disturb away, said Pereira, tell him it's the culture editor on the line. The editor-in-chief came to the tele-phone and said: Hello, chief editor here. Good morning sir, said Pereira, I have translated and edited a story by Balzac and there's enough of it for two or three issues, and I'm calling because I'd like to go for treatment at the thalassotherapeutic clinic at Parede, my heart condition is not improving and my doctor has advised this, do I have your permission? But what about the paper? asked the editor-in-chief. As I said sir, it is covered for at least two or three weeks, replied Pereira, and anyway I'll be a stone's throw from Lisbon and will leave you the telephone number of the clinic, and naturally if there's any trouble I'll hurry back to the office. But what about your assistant? said the editor-in-chief, could you not leave the assistant in charge? I would prefer not, replied Pereira, he has done me some obituaries but I'm not sure how serviceable they are, if some important writer dies I will look after it myself. Very well, said the editor-in-chief, take your week's treatment Dr. Pereira, after all there's the assistant editor at the main office and he can deal with any problems that might arise. Pereira said good-bye and asked to be remembered to the gracious lady whose acquaintance he had made. He hung up and glanced at his watch. It was almost time to start for the Café Orquídea, but first he wanted to read that anniversary article on D'Annunzio, which he hadn't had time for the previous evening. Pereira has kept it with him, so is in a position to produce it as evidence. It reads: "Exactly five months ago, at eight in the evening of March 1st 1938, died Gabriele D'Annunzio. At that time this newspaper did not have a culture page, but we are now in a position to speak of him. Was he a great poet, this Gabriele D'Annunzio whose real name incidentally was Rapagnetta? It is hard to give an answer, because we are his contemporaries and his works are still too fresh to us. Perhaps it makes better sense to speak of the figure of the man which intertwines with that of the artist. First and foremost, then, he was a Bard. He was also a lover of luxury, high society, magniloquence, action. He was a great decadent, a despoiler of the laws of morality, a devotee of the morbid and the erotic. From the German philosopher Nietzsche he inherited the myth of the superman, but he reduced it to the will to power of would-be aesthetic ideals which he exploited to construct the colorful kaleidoscope of a unique and inimitable career. In the Great War he was an interventionist, an implacable enemy of peace between nations. He achieved provocative feats of arms such as his flight over Vienna in 1918, when he scattered leaflets in Italian all over the city. After the war he organized the occupation of the city of Fiume, from which he was later expelled by Italian troops. Retiring to Gardone, to a villa which he himself named *Vittoriale degli Italiani*, he there led a dissolute and decadent life, marked by futile love affairs and erotic adventures. Fernando Pessoa nicknamed him *Trombone Solo* and maybe he had a point. Certainly the voice which comes over to us is not that of a delicate violin, but a brassy blare, a blustering trumpet. A life far from exemplary, a poet high-sounding and grandiose, a man much tarnished and compromised. Not an example to be followed, and it is for this very reason that we recall him here. Signed, Roxy."

Unpublishable, thought Pereira, completely unpublishable. He pulled out the file marked "Obituaries" and inserted the page. He has no idea why he did so, he could have simply thrown the thing away, but instead he filed it. Then, to get over the disgruntlement that had come over him, he decided to leave the office and make his way to the Café Orquídea.

When he reached the café the first thing he saw, Pereira maintains, was Marta's copper-colored hair. She was seated at a corner table near the fan, with her back to the door, and wearing the same dress as that evening at the Praça da Alegria, with shoulder straps crossed at the back. Pereira maintains he thought Marta's shoulders really lovely, finely molded, well-proportioned, perfect. He went over to join her. Oh, Dr. Pereira, said Marta serenely, I'm here instead of Monteiro Rossi, he couldn't come today.

Pereira took a seat at the table and asked Marta if she would like an aperitif. Marta said she would very much appreciate a glass of dry port. Pereira called the waiter and ordered two dry ports. He knew he ought not to drink alcohol, but after all he'd be going next day to the thalassotherapeutic clinic to diet for a week. Well? asked Pereira when the waiter had brought their drinks. Well, answered Marta, these are difficult times for all concerned, Monteiro Rossi has left for Alentejo and he'll be staying there for the time being, it's best for him to be out of Lisbon for a while. And his cousin? asked Pereira without thinking. Marta gave him a glance and smiled. Yes, I know you've been a great help to Monteiro Rossi and his cousin, said Marta, you've been really splendid, Dr. Pereira, you ought to be one of us. Pereira felt slightly nettled, he maintains, and took off his jacket. Listen Miss Marta, he protested, I am neither one of you nor one of them, I prefer to keep myself to myself, and in any case I don't know who you and yours are and don't wish to know, I am a journalist and my job is culture, I have just finished translating a story of Balzac's and as far as your business is concerned I prefer not to be in the know, I'm not a reporter. Marta took a sip of port and said: We're not providing fodder for the newspapers, Dr. Pereira, that's what I'd like to get across to you, we are living History. Pereira in turn took a sip of port and replied: Listen Miss Marta, History is a big word, I too have read Vico and Hegel in my time, and History is not the sort of animal you can domesticate. But perhaps you have not read Marx, objected Marta. No I haven't, said Pereira, and he doesn't interest me, I've had enough of the school of Hegel and let me repeat what I said before, that I think only about myself and culture, and that is my world. An anarcho-individualist? queried Marta, that's what I'd like to know. And what's that supposed to mean? demanded Pereira. Oh, said Marta, don't tell me you don't know the meaning of anarcho-individualist, Spain is full of them, the anarcho-individualists are getting a lot of attention at the moment and have actually done some heroic things, even if they could do with a bit more discipline, at least that's what I think. Look Marta, said Pereira, I haven't come to this café to talk politics, I already told you they leave me cold because I'm chiefly concerned with culture, I had an appointment with Monteiro Rossi and along you come and tell me he's in Alentejo, what's he gone to do in Alentejo?

Marta glanced round as if for the waiter. Shall we order something to eat? she asked, I have an appointment at three. Pereira summoned Manuel. They ordered two omelets *aux fines herbes* then Pereira repeated: So what has Monteiro Rossi gone to do in Alentejo? He's accompanying his cousin, replied Marta, his cousin got last-minute orders, it's mostly Alentejans who are raring to go and fight in Spain, there's a great democratic tradition in Alentejo, there are also a lot of anarcho-individualists like you, Dr. Pereira, there's plenty to do, and the fact is that Monteiro Rossi has had to take his cousin to Alentejo because that's where they're recruiting people. Very well, replied Pereira, I wish him good recruiting. The waiter brought the omelets and they started in on them. Pereira tied his table napkin round his neck, took a mouthful of omelet and then said: Look Marta, I'm leaving tomorrow for a thalassotherapeutic clinic near Cascais, I have health problems, tell Monteiro Rossi that his article on D'Annunzio is completely unusable, in any case I'll give you the number of the clinic where I'll be for a week, the best time to call me is at mealtimes, and now tell me where Monteiro Rossi is. Marta lowered her voice and said: Tonight he'll be at Portalegre with friends, but I'd rather not give you the address, and in any case it's very temporary because he sleeps a night here and a night there, he has to keep moving all over Alentejo, it'll most likely be him who'll get in touch with you. Very well, said Pereira, handing her a slip of paper, this is my telephone number at the thalassotherapeutic clinic at Parede.

I must be off, Dr. Pereira, said Marta, please excuse me but I have an appointment and I have to get right across town.

Pereira stood up and said good-bye. Marta put on her Italian straw hat as she walked away. Pereira watched her leave the café, he was entranced by that slender silhouette outlined against the sunlight. He felt greatly cheered, almost lighthearted, but had no idea why. Then he beckoned to Manuel who bustled up and asked if he would care for a liqueur. But he was thirsty, the afternoon was a scorcher. He pondered a moment, then said all he wanted was a lemonade. And he ordered it really cold, packed with ice, he maintains.

# FOURTEEN

Next day Pereira rose early, he maintains, drank some coffee, packed a small suitcase and slipped in Alphonse Daudet's *Contes du lundi*. He might possibly stay on a few days longer, he thought to himself, and Daudet was an author who would suit the *Lisboa* down to the ground.

Passing through the hall he paused in front of his wife's photograph and told it: Yesterday evening I saw Marta, Monteiro Rossi's fiancée, I have an idea those youngsters are getting themselves into really bad trouble, in fact they're already in it, in any case it's none of my business, I need a week of thalassotherapy, Dr. Costa has ordered it, and besides, Lisbon is stifling hot and I've translated Balzac's "Honorine," I'm leaving this morning, I'm just off to catch a train from Cais de Sodré and I'll take you with me if you don't mind. He picked up the photograph and laid it in his suitcase, face upwards, because his wife had all her life had such a need for air and he felt sure her picture also needed plenty of room to breathe. He made his way down to the cathedral square and waited for a taxi to take him to the station. Once there he thought he might have a bite to eat at the British Bar in the Cais de Sodré. He knew it was a place frequented by writers and he hoped to run across someone. In he went and sat down at a corner table. And sure enough there at the next table was Aquilino Ribeiro the novelist lunching with Bernardo Marques, the avant-garde artist who had designed and illustrated the leading Portuguese Modernist reviews. Pereira said good day and the two artists nodded in reply. It would be really something to lunch at their table, thought Pereira, to tell them how just yesterday he had received an article slamming D'Annunzio and to hear what they had to say about it. But the two men were talking ten to the dozen and Pereira couldn't pluck up courage to interrupt them. He gathered that Bernardo Marques intended to give up his art work and that the novelist had decided to go and live abroad. Pereira found this disheartening, he maintains, because he wouldn't have expected a writer of that caliber to go and leave his country in the lurch. While he drank his lemonade and picked away at a plate of periwinkles, Pereira overheard a few snatches. Paris, said Aquilino Ribeiro, the only conceivable place is Paris. Bernardo Marques nodded and said: I've had requests for work from several magazines, but I've got no incentive to go on drawing, this country is awful, it's better not to let anyone have one's work. Pereira finished his periwinkles and lemonade, got to his feet, and paused a moment by the table where the two artists sat. Gentlemen, don't let me interrupt your meal, he said, allow me to introduce myself however, I am Dr. Pereira of the culture page of *Lisboa*, the whole of Portugal is proud to have two such artists as you, we have sore need of you.

Then he went out into the blinding midday light and stepped across to the station. He bought a ticket to Parede and asked how long it took to get there. The clerk said no time at all sir and he felt thankful. It was the train for Estoril, used chiefly by vacationers. Pereira decided to sit on the left-hand side of the train because he wanted to look at the sea. The carriage was practically empty at that time of day so Pereira could sit anywhere he liked. He lowered the blind a little because his window faced south and the sun was in his eyes. And he sat looking out at the sea. His thoughts turned to his past life, but he has no wish to talk about that, he maintains. He prefers simply to say that the sea was calm and there were bathers on the beach. Pereira thought how long it was since he had last swum in the sea, it seemed centuries ago. He remembered his days at Coimbra, when he used to haunt the beaches near

Oporto, Granja for example, or Espinho, where they had a casino and a club. The sea was freezing cold on those northerly beaches, but he was quite capable of swimming all morning long, while his fellow undergraduates, chilled to the marrow, waited for him on the beach. Eventually they would all get dressed, put on smart jackets and go to the club to play billiards. People would stare at them as they came in and the headwaiter would greet them crying: Here come our students from Coimbra! And he would give them the best billiard table.

Pereira came out of his reverie when they were drawing level with Santo Amaro. The beach was a splendid curve dotted with blue-and-white-striped canvas bathing huts. The train came to a halt and Pereira was seized with the notion of getting out and having a swim, he could always go on by the next train. The impulse was too strong for him. Pereira cannot presume to say why he felt it, perhaps it was because he had been thinking of his Coimbra days and swimming at Granja. So he left the train, carrying his little suitcase, and went down through the tunnel leading to the beach. On reaching the sand he took off his shoes and socks and continued barefoot, his case in one hand and his shoes in the other. He spotted the bathing attendant at once, a bronzed young man keeping an eye on the bathers while lolling in a deckchair. Pereira told him he wanted to hire a bathing suit and a changing hut. The attendant sneakily looked him up and down and murmured: I don't know that we have a costume your size, but I'll give you the key of the storeroom and cabin number one, which is the roomiest. He then inquired in a tone which to Pereira sounded like a snub: Would you be wanting a rubber ring as well? I'm a very good swimmer, replied Pereira, perhaps a lot better than you are yourself, so don't worry. He took the keys of the storeroom and the cabin and went off. In the storeroom he found a bit of everything: buoys, inflatable rings, a fishing net festooned with corks, and bathing suits. He rummaged among the latter to see if there was an old-fashioned, one-piece suit that would cover his paunch. Luckily he found one and tried it on. It was woolen and on the tight side, but still the best of the bunch. His suitcase and clothes he dumped in the changing hut and then walked down the beach. At the water's edge were a number of young men playing ball and Pereira gave them a wide berth. He entered the water slowly, by degrees, allowing its coolness to envelop him little by little. Then, when the water was up to his belly button, in he plunged and began to swim a slow, measured crawl. He swam a long way, right out to the line of buoys. As soon as he caught hold of a buoy he realized he was completely winded and that his heart was thumping madly. I'm crazy, he thought, I haven't swum for half a lifetime and here I go throwing myself into the water like an athlete. He clung to the buoy and rested awhile, then turned onto his back and floated. The sky above him was so blue it was wounding to the eyes. Pereira caught his breath and returned with slow strokes leisurely to shore. As he passed the attendant it occurred to him he might get a bit of his own back. Maybe you noticed I didn't need a ring, he said, but can you tell me the time of the next train for Estoril? The attendant consulted his watch. In fifteen minutes, he replied. Fine, said Pereira, in that case I'll go and dress and you come along to the hut to be paid because I don't have much time. He dressed, came out, combed what little hair he had left with a pocket comb he kept in his wallet, and paid the attendant. Good-bye, he said, and I advise you to keep an eye on those boys playing ball, in my opinion they're a nuisance to the rest of us and can't swim anyway.

He hurried through the tunnel and sat down on a stone bench under the awning. He heard the train approaching and glanced at his watch. It occurred to him that it was pretty late, at the thalassotherapeutic clinic they had probably expected him for lunch, and they eat early in such places. Never mind, he thought. He had a healthy glow, he felt fresh and relaxed as the train drew in to the platform, and anyway, he maintains, he was in no hurry to get to the thalassotherapeutic clinic, he would be staying there at least a week.

When he arrived at Parede it was almost half past two. He hailed a taxi and asked the driver to take him to the thalassotherapeutic clinic. The one for tuberculars? asked the driver. I don't know, said Pereira, but it's on the sea. Then it's only just down the road, said the driver, you'd just as well walk there. Look here, said Pereira, it's very hot and I'm tired and I'll give you a good tip.

The thalassotherapeutic clinic was a pink building surrounded by a large garden full of palm trees. It was perched high on the rocks with a flight of steps leading down to the road and continuing on to the beach. Pereira toiled up the steps and entered the lobby. There he was received by a fat, white-coated lady with a florid complexion. I am Dr. Pereira, said Pereira, I believe my doctor, Dr. Costa, has telephoned to book a room for me. Oh, Dr. Pereira, said the white-coated lady, why are you so late, we were expecting you for lunch, have you had any? To tell the truth all I've had is some periwinkles at the station, confessed Pereira, and I feel quite peckish. Then come along with me, said the white-coated lady, the restaurant is closed but Maria das Dores is still on duty and she'll make you a snack. She piloted him as far as the dining room, a vast apartment with big windows overlooking the sea. It was completely deserted. Pereira sat down at a table and along came a heavily mustachioed woman in an apron. I am Maria das Dores, said the woman, I'm the cook here, I can do you a little grilled something. A sole, replied Pereira, many thanks. At the same time he ordered a lemonade and soon began to sip it with relish. He removed his jacket and spread the table napkin over his shirt. Maria das Dores arrived with a grilled fish. We're out of sole, she said, but I've done you a bream. Pereira set to with gusto. The seaweed baths are at five o'clock, said the cook, but if you don't feel up to it and want to have a snooze you can start tomorrow, your doctor is Dr. Cardoso, he'll visit you in your room at six. Perfect, said Pereira, I think I'll go and lie down for a bit.

He went up to his room, number twenty-two, and found his suitcase already there. He closed the shutters, brushed his teeth and slipped between the sheets in his birthday suit. A fine fresh breeze off the Atlantic was filtering through the slats of the shutters and stirring the curtains. Pereira fell asleep almost at once. And he dreamed a lovely dream, a dream of his youth. He was at the beach at Granja, swimming in an ocean for all the world like a swimming pool, and on the edge of the pool was a pale-skinned girl, waiting for him and clasping a towel in her arms. Then he swam back, but the dream went on, it was really a beautiful dream. But Pereira prefers not to say how it went on because his dream has nothing to do with these events, he maintains.

# FIFTEEN

At half past six Pereira heard a knock at the door, though he was awake in any case, he maintains, and was gazing up at the ceiling, at the strips of light and shadow cast by the shutters, thinking of Balzac's "Honorine," and of repentance. And he felt he had something to repent of but he didn't know what. He had a sudden longing to talk to Father António, because to him he'd have been able to confide that he wanted to repent but didn't know what he had to repent of, he only felt a yearning for repentance as such, surely that's what he meant, or perhaps (who knows?) he simply liked the idea of repentance.

Who is it? called Pereira. It's time for your constitutional, came a nurse's voice from outside the door, Dr. Cardoso is waiting for you in the lobby. Pereira had not the slightest desire to take a constitutional, he maintains, but he got up all the same, opened his case, put on some cotton trousers, a roomy khaki shirt, and a pair of espadrilles. He took his wife's photograph, propped it up on the table and told it: Well, here I am at the thalassotherapeutic clinic, but if I get bored I'll leave, luckily I brought a book by Alphonse Daudet so I can do some translations for the paper, our favorite of Daudet's was "Le petit chose," d'you remember? we read it at Coimbra and we both found it really touching, it's a story of childhood, and perhaps we were thinking of a child that never came our way, well never mind, anyway I've brought the *Contes du lundi*, I think that one of those stories would do very well for the *Lisboa*, but you must excuse me now, I have to go, it seems there's a doctor waiting to see me, we'll soon find out what this thalassotherapy is all about, so I'll see you later.

On reaching the lobby he saw a white-coated figure looking out at the sea. Pereira went up to him. He was a man between thirty-five and forty, with blue eyes and a little blond beard. Good evening, said the doctor with an unassuming smile, I am Dr. Cardoso, you must be Dr. Pereira, it's time for the patients to go for their walk along the beach, but if you prefer we can stay and talk here or in the garden. Pereira replied that he didn't much care for a walk on the beach, he said he'd already been on the beach that day, and gave him an account of his swim at Santo Amaro. Oh, that's really good news, said Dr. Cardoso, I thought I had a more difficult case on my hands, but I see that you are still drawn to outdoor life. Perhaps it's truer to say that I'm drawn to memories, said Pereira. How do you mean? asked Dr. Cardoso. I'll explain in due course, said Pereira, not now, perhaps tomorrow.

They went out into the garden. Shall we take a stroll? suggested Dr. Cardoso, it would do you good and me as well. Beyond the palm trees in the garden, which grew amid rocks and sand, there was a fine greensward dotted with trees. Dr. Cardoso, who seemed in a chatty mood, led the way there. You've been placed under my care during your stay, said the doctor, so I need to talk to you, to learn about your way of life, you must have no secrets from me. Ask me anything you like, said Pereira readily. Dr. Cardoso plucked a blade of grass and started chewing on it. Let's start with your eating habits, he said, what are they? First thing in the morning I have coffee, replied Pereira, then I have lunch and supper like everyone else, that's all there is to it. But what dietary regimen do you maintain, asked Dr. Cardoso, I mean what do you usually eat? Omelets, Pereira would have liked to answer, I eat almost nothing but omelets, because my caretaker makes me omelet sandwiches and because all they serve at the Café Orquídea is omelets *aux fines herbes*. But he was too ashamed, and gave a quite different answer. A varied diet, said he, fish, meat, vegetables. I'm a fairly frugal eater and arrange these matters rationally. And when did you first begin to suffer from obesity? asked Dr. Cardoso. Some years ago, replied Pereira, after my wife died. And what about sweets, asked Dr. Cardoso, do you eat a lot of sweet things? Never touch them, replied Pereira, I don't like them, I only drink lemonade. What sort of lemonade? asked Dr. Cardoso. Freshly squeezed lemon juice, said Pereira, I like it, I find it refreshing and I really feel that it does my insides good, because I often have trouble with my insides. How many glasses a day? asked Dr. Cardoso. Pereira reflected a moment. It depends on the day, he replied, these hot summer days, for example, ten or a dozen. Ten or a dozen lemonades a day! exclaimed Dr. Cardoso, my dear Dr. Pereira, that seems to me madness, and tell me, do you take sugar in it? Masses of sugar, said Pereira, half a glass of lemon juice and half of sugar. Dr. Cardoso spat the blade of grass from the tip of his tongue, raised a stern hand and pronounced: From today on no more lemonades, you will drink mineral water instead, preferably not effervescent, but if you prefer it bubbly that is also acceptable. There was a bench under the cedar trees and Pereira sat himself down on it, obliging Dr. Cardoso to do likewise. I'm sure you'll forgive me, Dr. Pereira, said Dr. Cardoso, but now I have to ask an intimate question: What about sexual activity? Pereira lofted his gaze to the treetops and said: What exactly do you mean? Women, explained Dr. Cardoso, do you sleep with women, do you have a regular sex life? Look here doctor, said Pereira, I'm a widower, I'm no longer young and I have an exacting job, I have neither the time nor the inclination to go chasing after women. Not even from time to time? asked Dr. Cardoso, I mean not even a chance affair, some obliging lady every so often? Not even that, said Pereira, pulling out a cigar and asking permission to smoke. Dr. Cardoso nodded. It's not good for your heart, he said, but if you must you must. It's because your questions embarrass me, confessed Pereira. Well here comes another embarrassing question, said Dr. Cardoso, do you have wet dreams? I don't understand the question, said Pereira. What I mean, said Dr. Cardoso, is do you have erotic dreams that lead to orgasm, do you have erotic dreams at all, what do you dream about? Listen doctor, replied Pereira, my father taught me that our dreams are the most private and personal thing we have and we should never reveal them to anyone. But you're here for treatment and I'm your doctor, objected Dr. Cardoso, your psyche is part and parcel with your body and I absolutely must know what you dream about. I often dream of Granja, confessed Pereira. Is that a woman? asked Dr. Cardoso. It's a place, said Pereira, it's a beach near Oporto, I used to go there as a young man when I was a student at Coimbra, and there was also Espinho, a classy beach with a swimming pool and casino, I often used to have a swim there and then a game of billiards, there was a first-rate billiard room, and that's where I and my fiancée whom I later married used to go, she was a sick woman though she didn't know it yet, she just suffered from bad head-aches, that was a wonderful time in my life, and maybe I dream about it because it gives me pleasure to dream about it. Very good, said Dr. Cardoso, that'll do for today, though I'd very much like to join you for dinner if I may, it'll give us a chance to chat about this and that, I'm very fond of literature and I've noticed that your paper gives a lot of space to French writers of the last century, and I studied in Paris, you know, I'm French-trained, and this evening I'll outline the program for tomorrow, we'll meet in the restaurant at eight o'clock.

Dr. Cardoso got up and said good-bye for now. Pereira remained seated and took another look at the treetops. Excuse me doctor, he said, you know I promised to stub out my cigar but now I find I want to finish it. Do as you wish, said Dr. Cardoso, we'll start your diet tomorrow. Pereira sat on alone and smoked. He couldn't help thinking that Dr. Costa, who was after all an old acquaintance, would never have asked him such personal, intimate questions, evidently young doctors who had studied in Paris had quite different ideas. Pereira was astonished looking back on it and felt terribly embarrassed, but he decided it was better not to think too much about it, he maintains, this was plainly a queer sort of clinic.

# SIXTEEN

By eight o'clock on the dot Dr. Cardoso was seated in the restaurant. Pereira also arrived on time, he maintains, and before making his way to their table, wearing his gray suit and black tie, he stood for a moment taking in the scene. There were about fifty people in the room, all of them older than him, he was pretty certain of that, mostly elderly couples dining at tables for two. The thought that he was one of the youngest there made him feel a bit better, he maintains, it bucked him up to think he wasn't that old after all. Dr. Cardoso gave him a smile and began to get to his feet, but Pereira held up a restraining hand. Well Dr. Cardoso, said Pereira, I am in your hands as regards this meal as well. In that case a glass of mineral water on an empty stomach is always a good rule of health, said Dr. Cardoso. Fizzy, pleaded Pereira. Fizzy let it be then, conceded Dr. Cardoso, and he filled his glass for him. Pereira drank it down, felt slightly sick, and longed for a lemonade. Dr. Pereira, said Dr. Cardoso, I'd be interested to know your future plans for the culture page of the *Lisboa*, I really enjoyed the anniversary article on Pessoa, and also the Maupassant story (extremely well-translated, incidentally). I translated it myself, admitted Pereira, but I don't care to sign my work. You're wrong there, said Dr. Cardoso, you ought to sign it, especially the best pieces, but what does your paper have up its sleeve for us now? As things stand, Dr. Cardoso, said Pereira, for the next three or four issues there's a story by Balzac, it's called "Honorine," I wonder if you know it. Dr. Cardoso shook his head. It's a story about repentance, said Pereira, a beautiful story that has to do with repentance, so much so that I read it as autobiography. What! our great Balzac repented! exclaimed Dr. Cardoso. Pereira was silent for a moment, wrapped in thought, then: Forgive me for asking, Dr. Cardoso, he said, but you told me earlier this evening that you got your degree in France, what exactly did you get it in, if I may ask? I qualified in medicine and then specialized in two fields, dietology and psychology, replied Dr. Cardoso. I don't see the connection between the two, said Pereira, please forgive me but I simply don't see it. There may be more connection than most people think, said Dr. Cardoso, I don't know if you can begin to conceive the interplay between our bodies and our psyches, there's a lot more of it than I think you realize, but you were telling me that this story of Balzac's is an autobiographical story. Oh that's not what I meant at all, replied Pereira, I meant that I read it as having a bearing on myself, that I recognized myself in it. In the repentance? asked Dr. Cardoso. Yes, said Pereira, I did in a way, even if rather obliquely, or perhaps marginally is the word I want, let's say that I recognized myself marginally.

Dr. Cardoso beckoned to the waitress. Let's have fish this evening, said Dr. Cardoso, I would rather you had it grilled or boiled, but you can have it some other way if you like. I had grilled fish for lunch, pleaded Pereira, and plain boiled it really doesn't appeal to me, it smacks too much of hospitals and I don't like to think of myself as being in a hospital, I prefer to think I'm in a hotel, what I'd really like would be a sole meunière. Perfect, said Dr. Cardoso, sole meunière with buttered carrots, I'll join you. Then he came right back to the subject and said: What exactly is marginal repentance? Well, your having studied psychology makes it easier for me to talk to you, said Pereira, perhaps I'd do even better to discuss it with my friend Father António, who after all is a priest, but then again he might not understand, because priests are people we have to confess our sins to, and I don't feel guilty of anything in particular, I just have this desire for repentance, I feel a real yearning for repentance. Maybe you ought to go more deeply into the matter, Dr. Pereira, said Dr. Cardoso, and if you care to do so with me I am at your service. Well, said Pereira, it's a strange sort of feeling there on the very edge of myself, and that's why I call it marginal, the fact is that on the one hand I'm happy to have lived the life I have, happy to have taken my degree at Coimbra, to have married a sick woman who spent her life in and out of sanatoriums, to have been a crime reporter for so many years on a leading paper and finally to have accepted this job of editing the culture page of a second-rate evening paper, and yet at the same time it's as if I had an urge to repent of my life, if you see what I mean.

Dr. Cardoso took a forkful of sole meunière and Pereira followed suit. I would need to know more about these last few months of your life, said Dr. Cardoso, perhaps there has been some event. Event in what sense, asked Pereira, how exactly do you mean? Event is a term used in psychoanalysis, said Dr. Cardoso, personally I don't believe all that much in Freud because I'm a syncretist, but I do believe that on this question of the event he is certainly right, and by an event he means something that actually happens in our lives to upset or disturb our convictions and peace of mind, in short an event is something which occurs in our everyday life and has an impact on the life of our psyche, and I am asking you to consider whether there has not recently been such a thing in your own life. Yes, said Pereira, I have met someone, in fact two people, a young man and a girl. Tell me about them, said Dr. Cardoso. Well, said Pereira, the fact is that for my culture page I needed advance obituaries of any leading writers who might possibly die, and the person in question had written a thesis on death, it's true that he copied some of it, but it seemed to me at first that he understood what death is all about, so I took him on as an assistant to do the advance obituaries, and he actually has done a few, and I've paid him out of my own pocket because I haven't wanted to charge it to the *Lisboa*, but his stuff is all unpublishable, because that boy has his head full of politics and writes every obituary thinking of nothing but politics, though honestly I think it's his girl who's putting these ideas into his head, you know, fascism, socialism, civil war in Spain and things of that sort, and they're all unpublishable articles as I said, and so far I've paid him out of my own pocket. There's no harm in that, said Dr. Cardoso, after all you're only risking your own cash. That's not the point, stated Pereira, the fact is that I've been stricken with misgiving, what I mean is what if those two youngsters are right? In that case they're right, said Dr. Cardoso gently, but that's for History to say, not you, Dr. Pereira. True enough, said Pereira, but if they were right my life wouldn't make any sense, it wouldn't make any sense to have read literature at Coimbra and always thought that literature was the most important thing in the world, there'd be no sense in my editing the culture page of this evening rag where I can't say what I want to say and have to publish nineteenth-century French stories, in fact nothing would make any sense at all, and this is why I feel I need to repent, just as if I were someone else entirely, and not the Pereira who's spent all his working life as a journalist, and it's as if there were something I had to apologize for.

Dr. Cardoso beckoned the waitress and ordered two fruit salads, no sugar or ice cream please. Then: I have a question for you, said Dr. Cardoso, and that is, are you acquainted with the *médecins-philosophes*? No I'm not, admitted Pereira, who are they? The leaders of this school of thought are Théodule Ribot and Pierre Janet, said Dr. Cardoso, it was their work I studied in Paris, they are doctors and psychologists, but also philosophers, and they hold a theory I think interesting, the theory of the confederation of souls. Tell me about it, said Pereira. Well, said Dr. Cardoso, it means that to believe in a "self" as a distinct entity, quite distinct from the infinite variety of all the other "selves" that we have within us, is a fallacy, the naive illusion of the single unique soul we inherit from Christian tradition, whereas Dr. Ribot and Dr. Janet see the personality as a confederation of numerous souls, because within us we each have numerous souls, don't you think, a confederation which agrees to put itself under the government of one ruling ego. Dr. Cardoso made a brief pause and then continued: What we think of as ourselves, our inward being, is only an effect, not a cause, and what's more it is subject to the control of a ruling ego which has imposed its will on the confederation of our souls, so in the case of another ego arising, one stronger and more powerful, this ego overthrows the first ruling ego, takes its place and rules over the cohort of souls, or rather the confederation, and remains in power until it is in turn overthrown by yet another ruling ego, either by frontal attack or by slow nibbling away. It may be, concluded Dr. Cardoso, that after slowly nibbling away in you some ruling ego is gaining command of your confederation of souls, Dr. Pereira, and there's nothing you can do about it except perhaps give it a helping hand whenever you get the chance.

Dr. Cardoso finished his fruit salad and dabbed his lips on his napkin. So what do you suggest I should do? asked Pereira. Nothing, replied Dr. Cardoso, just wait, perhaps after this slow nibbling away, after all these years you've spent in journalism working on crime cases and thinking that literature is all the world to you, there's a new ruling ego taking over the leadership of your confederation of souls, and you must let it come to the surface, there's really no other way out, you wouldn't bring it off and you'd only come into conflict with yourself, so if you wish to repent of your life go ahead and repent, and if you wish to tell a priest go ahead and tell him, and in a word, Dr. Pereira, if you're beginning to think that those youngsters are in the right and that your life up to now has been worthless, go ahead and think it, perhaps from now on your life will no longer seem worthless, let yourself be guided by your new ruling ego and don't go compensating for the pain it gives you by stuffing yourself and guzzling lemonade filled with sugar.

Pereira finished his fruit salad and untied the napkin from around his neck. It's very interesting, this theory of yours, he said, I'll think it over, I'd like a cup of coffee now, if that's all right with you? Coffee induces insomnia, said Dr. Cardoso, but if you don't wish to sleep that's up to you, the seaweed baths take place twice a day, at nine in the morning and five in the afternoon, I'd like you to be on time tomorrow morning, I'm sure a seaweed bath will do you a lot of good.

Goodnight then, mumbled Pereira. He got up to leave, took a step or two, then turned. Dr. Cardoso was smiling at him, and Pereira promised he'd be there on the dot of nine, he maintains.

# SEVENTEEN

At nine o'clock next morning, Pereira maintains, he made his way down the steps to the private beach of the clinic. In the reef bordering the beach two huge pools had been hacked out of the living rock, where the ocean waves washed in on their own sweet time. The pools were full of long fronds of seaweed, plump and glossy, floating on the surface where a number of patients were wallowing about. Beside the pools were two wooden huts, painted blue, evidently the changing rooms. Pereira spotted Dr. Cardoso keeping an eye on the patients immersed in the pools and teaching them the right movements to make. Pereira went up and said good morning. He was in fine fettle, he maintains, and really felt the urge to get into those pools even though it was pretty chilly there on the rocks and maybe the water temperature was not ideal for a dip. He asked Dr. Cardoso for the loan of a swimsuit because, he said apologetically, he had neglected to bring one with him, and asked if possible for an old-fashioned one, of the kind that cover the stomach and part of the chest. Dr. Cardoso shook his head. I'm sorry, Dr. Pereira, he said, but you'll have to get over your blushes, the beneficent effects of the seaweed act chiefly by contact with the skin, they have to massage the belly and chest, you'll have to wear trunks. Pereira resigned himself and went to the changing hut. He left his trousers and khaki shirt on a peg and emerged again. The air was cool with a vengeance, but bracing. Pereira tested the water with one foot and found it not as icy as he had expected. He got in to the water gingerly, shuddering slightly as those strands of seaweed stuck to him all over. Dr. Cardoso came to the edge of the pool and started to give him instructions. Move your arms as if you were doing physical jerks, he said, and massage your stomach and chest with the seaweed. Pereira carried out the instructions to the letter until he found his breath coming short. Whereupon he stopped, stood with the water up to his neck and began to make slow circling movements with his hands. How did you sleep? asked Dr. Cardoso. Very well indeed, replied Pereira, but I read until late, I brought along a book by Alphonse Daudet, do you like Daudet? I know him very little, admitted Dr. Cardoso. I've been thinking of translating a story from the *Contes du lundi*, I'd like to publish it in the *Lisboa*, said Pereira. Tell me the story, said Dr. Cardoso. Well, said Pereira, it's called "La dernière classe," it's about the schoolmaster of a French village in Alsace, his pupils are all sons of peasants, poor boys who have to work in the fields so they seldom come to lessons and the teacher is driven to despair. Pereira took a few steps forward so that the water stopped slopping into his mouth, and went on: Finally comes the last day of school, the Franco-Prussian War has just ended, the teacher waits without much hope for some pupil to show up, but who should he see instead but every man jack in the village, the peasants, the village elders, all coming to pay homage to their French schoolmaster who is going to have to leave them, for they know that next day their school will be occupied by the Germans, so the teacher writes up on the blackboard "*Vive la France!*" and off he goes, with tears in his eyes, leaving a tumult of emotion behind him in the schoolroom. Pereira peeled two long strands of seaweed off his arms and asked: How does it strike you, Dr. Cardoso? Great stuff, replied Dr. Cardoso, but I'm not sure that many people in Portugal today will much appreciate reading "*Vive la France!*," seeing the times we live in, and I wonder if you're not making room for your new ruling ego, Dr. Pereira, I seem to catch a glimpse of a new ruling ego. Oh come now, Dr. Cardoso, said Pereira, this is a nineteenth-century story, it's ancient history. That's true, said Dr. Cardoso, but none the less it's an anti-German story, and Germany is above criticism in a country like ours today, have you seen the salute they've made compulsory at official functions, they make the stiff-armed salute like the Nazis. That may be so, said Pereira, but the *Lisboa* is an independent newspaper. Then he asked: Please can I get out now? Another ten minutes, replied Dr. Cardoso, now that you're in you'd better stay in for the full time required by the therapy, and forgive me for asking but exactly what is an independent newspaper these days in Portugal? A newspaper not connected with any political movement, replied Pereira. That's as may be, said Dr. Cardoso, but the editor of your paper, my dear Dr. Pereira, is a supporter of the regime, he appears at every official function, and from the way he flings out his arm you'd think he was throwing the javelin. True, conceded Pereira, but he's not a bad fellow at heart, and as regards the culture page he's given me a free hand. No skin off his nose, retorted Dr. Cardoso, because there's the state censorship and every day, before your paper appears, the proofs are examined by the censors, and if there's something they don't like, don't you worry, it won't be printed, they leave blank spaces, I've already seen Portuguese papers with huge blank spaces in them, and it makes me very angry and very sad. I know, I know, said Pereira, I've seen them too, however it hasn't yet happened to the *Lisboa*. But it might happen, said Dr. Cardoso almost teasingly, it all depends on the ruling ego that gains the upper hand in your confederation of souls. Then he went on: Do you know what I think, Dr. Pereira, if you want to help the ruling ego that's beginning to peep out perhaps you ought to live somewhere else, leave this country, I think you would have fewer conflicts with yourself, after all there's nothing to prevent you, you're a serious professional man, you speak good French, you're a widower, you have no children, what ties do you have to this country? My whole past life, replied Pereira, my precious memories, and you, Dr. Cardoso, why don't you go back to France? after all you studied there, you had a French education. It's by no means out of the question, replied Dr. Cardoso, I am in touch with a thalassotherapeutic clinic at Saint-Malo, and might decide to go at any moment. May I get out now? asked Pereira. How time has passed without our noticing it, said Dr. Cardoso, you've been under treatment a quarter of an hour longer than necessary, by all means go and get dressed, what would you say to lunching together? With pleasure, said Pereira.

That day Pereira had Dr. Cardoso's company for lunch and on his advice, he maintains, ate boiled hake. They talked about literature, Maupassant and Daudet, and about France, what a great country it was. Afterwards Pereira retired to his room and had a short nap, just fifteen minutes, then he lay and watched the strips of light and shadow cast on the ceiling by the shutters. In midafternoon he got up, had a shower, put on his black tie and sat down in front of his wife's photograph. I've found an intelligent doctor, he confided to it, his name is Cardoso, he studied in France, he has told me a theory of his about the human soul, or rather, it's a French philosophical theory, it seems that inside us we have a confederation of souls and every so often a ruling ego comes along and takes over the leadership of the confederation, Dr. Cardoso suggests that I'm changing my ruling ego, as snakes change their skins, and that this new ruling ego will change my life, I don't know how true this is and in fact I'm not all that convinced, but never mind, we must wait and see.

Then he sat down at the table and began translating "La dernière classe" by Daudet. He had brought along his Larousse, which made things easy for him. But he only translated one page, because he didn't want to rush it, and because that story kept him company. And in fact throughout the week Pereira stayed at the thalassotherapeutic clinic he spent every afternoon translating Daudet's story, he maintains.

It was a wonderful week of therapy, relaxation and dieting, cheered by the presence of Dr. Cardoso, with whom he always had lively and interesting talks, especially about literature. A week that slipped by in the twinkling of an eye, on the Saturday the first installment of Balzac's "Honorine" came out in the *Lisboa* and Dr. Cardoso complimented him on it. The editor-in-chief never called him, which meant that all was running smoothly at the paper. There was no sign of Monteiro Rossi either, or of Marta. In his last few days there Pereira scarcely gave them a thought. And when he left the clinic to take the train back to Lisbon he felt like a new man, in tip-top shape, he had lost nine pounds, he maintains.

# EIGHTEEN

Pereira returned to Lisbon, and the better part of August vanished almost before he could look round, he maintains. Piedade, his maid-of-all-work, was not yet back, but in his mailbox he found a card from her, postmarked Setúbal, which read: "Returning mid-September because my sister has to have operation for varicose veins, all the best, Piedade."

Pereira settled back into his flat. Luckily the weather had changed and it wasn't all that hot. In the evening a stiffish Atlantic breeze would spring up, so he had to wear a jacket. When he went back to the office he found few changes. The caretaker was no longer huffy with him, in fact she was a good deal more friendly, but a horrible stench of frying still hung about on the landing. There wasn't much in the way of mail: the electricity bill, which he forwarded to the main office, and a letter postmarked Chaves, from a lady in her fifties who wrote children's stories and was hereby submitting one to the *Lisboa*. It was a tale of elves and fairies which had nothing whatever to do with Portugal and which the author must have filched from some Irish story. Pereira wrote her a courteous answer suggesting that she should base her work on Portuguese folklore, because, he told her, the *Lisboa* was addressed to Portuguese, not to English-speaking readers. Towards the end of the month a letter arrived from Spain. It was addressed to Monteiro Rossi, and the envelope read: Señor Monteiro Rossi, c/o Dr. Pereira, Rua Rodrigo da Fonseca 66, Lisbon, Portugal. Pereira was tempted to open it. He had practically forgotten Monteiro Rossi, or at least so he thought, and he found it beyond belief that the young man should have told anyone to address a letter to him c/o the culture page of the *Lisboa*. However, he put it unopened into the "Obituaries" file. He then had lunch at the Café Orquídea, though he didn't order omelets *aux fines herbes*, because Dr. Cardoso had forbidden them, and he no longer drank lemonade. Instead he ate seafood salad and drank mineral water. Balzac's "Honorine" had been published in its entirety and had been a great success with the readers. Pereira maintains that he even received two telegrams, one from Tavira and the other from Estremoz, the first saying that it was a really marvelous story and the other that repentance is a thing we all ought to think about, and both of them ending with the words: Thank you. It occurred to Pereira that perhaps someone had received the message in the bottle, and he set about preparing the final draft of Daudet's "La dernière classe." The editor-in-chief called him one morning to congratulate him on the Balzac story, saying that the head office had been simply inundated with compliments. Pereira had a feeling that the editor-in-chief would never receive the message in the bottle, and he chortled to himself. That message was really and truly a coded message, and only people who had ears to hear could receive it. The editor-in-chief did not have ears to hear and could not receive it. So now, Dr. Pereira, asked the editor-in-chief, what have you got up your sleeve for us? I have just finished translating a story by Daudet, replied Pereira, I hope it will be suitable. I trust it isn't "L'Arlésienne," said the editor-in-chief, glad to be able to show off one of his few scraps of literary knowledge, that story is a bit *osé*, and I don't think it would go down well with our readers. Pereira simply said: No, it's a tale from the *Contes du lundi*, it's called "The Last Class," I wonder if you know it, it's a story about love of one's country. I don't know it, replied the editor-in-chief, but if it's a patriotic story that's all to the good, we all need patriotism in this day and age, patriotism is just the ticket. Pereira said good-bye and hung up. He had scarcely gathered up the typescript to take it to the printer's when the telephone rang again. Pereira was at the door already with his jacket on. Hello, said a woman's voice, good morning Dr. Pereira, this is Marta, I would like to see you. Pereira's heart missed a beat and then he asked: How are you, Marta, and how is Monteiro Rossi? I'll tell you in due course, Dr. Pereira, said Marta, where can I meet you this evening? Pereira considered for a moment and was on the point of telling her to come to his place, then thought better of it and answered: At the Café Orquídea at half past eight. All right, said Marta, I've cut my hair short and bleached it, I'll see you at the Café Orquídea at half past eight, however Monteiro Rossi is well and is sending you an article.

Leaving the office to go to the printer's Pereira felt uneasy, he maintains. He thought of going back to the office and waiting there until it was time for dinner, but he then realized what he absolutely must do was go home and have a cold bath. He therefore took a taxi and made the cabbie drive all the way up the steep slope to his house. Taxi drivers usually refused to go up that ramp because it was hard to turn at the top, so Pereira had to promise a tip, he was quite worn out, he maintains. He entered his flat and the first thing he did was run a cold bath. He lay in it and gently massaged his paunch as Dr. Cardoso had taught him to. Then he put on his bathrobe, went into the hall and addressed his wife's portrait. Marta is on the scene again, he informed it, she tells me she's cut her hair short and bleached it, I don't know why, and she's bringing me an article by Monteiro Rossi, but Monteiro Rossi is evidently still off on business of his own, those kids worry me but never mind, I'll tell you how things go by and by.

At eight thirty-five, Pereira maintains, he entered the Café Orquídea. The only reason he recognized Marta in the skinny little shrimp with cropped hair sitting near the fan was that she was wearing the same dress as ever, otherwise he would never have taken her for the same girl. She seemed like another person,

Marta did, with that cropped bleached hair and the fringe and the wisps curving forward over her ears, giving her a tomboy, rather foreign look, rather French, perhaps. What's more, she must have lost at least twenty pounds. Of her shoulders, which Pereira remembered as so soft and shapely, there now remained two bony shoulder blades that stuck out like the wings of a plucked chicken. Pereira sat down opposite her and said: Good evening Marta, what on earth has happened to you? I decided to change my appearance, replied Marta, in certain circumstances it's necessary and in my case it became essential to make myself a different person.

Heaven knows why it occurred to Pereira to ask her a certain question. He cannot begin to say why he did it. Perhaps because she was too blonde and too unnatural and he could hardly recognize her as the girl he had known, perhaps because every so often she gave a furtive glance around as if expecting someone or afraid of something, but the fact is that he asked her: Is your name still Marta? To you I am Marta, of course, replied Marta, but I have a French passport, my name is Lise Delaunay, I am a painter by profession and am in Portugal to paint watercolor landscapes, though the real reason is simply travel.

Pereira felt a terrific urge to order an omelet *aux fines herbes* and a glass of lemonade, he maintains. What would you say to a couple of omelets *aux fines herbes*? he asked Marta. With pleasure, replied Marta, but first I'd really like a glass of dry port. So would I, said Pereira, and ordered two dry ports. I sense trouble, said Pereira, you're in a pickle Marta, you might as well admit it. I don't deny it, answered Marta, but it's the kind of trouble I like, I feel in my element, after all it's the life I've chosen. Pereira shrugged his shoulders. Just as long as you're happy, he said, and Monteiro Rossi, he's in trouble too I imagine, because he hasn't been in touch, what's happening to him? I can tell you about myself but not about Monteiro Rossi, said Marta, I can answer only for myself, he hasn't been in touch with you so far because he's been in difficulties, he'll still be out of Lisbon for a while, he's on the move in Alentejo, his problems may be bigger than mine, in any case he's short of money into the bargain and that's why he's sent you this article, he says it's an anniversary article, you can give me the money if you like and I'll see that he gets it.

Pereira would have liked to say: Don't speak to me of those articles of his, obituaries or anniversaries it makes no difference, all I do is pay Monteiro Rossi out of my own pocket, I still don't know why I don't fire him, I offered him a job as a journalist, I gave him a chance of a career. But he uttered not a word of all this. Instead he took out his wallet and extracted two banknotes. Give him this from me, he said, and now let's have the article. Marta took a sheet of paper from her handbag and handed it over. See here Marta, said Pereira, I'd like you to know there are certain things you can count on me for, even if I'd prefer to steer clear of your problems, as you know I don't concern myself with politics, however if you hear from Monteiro Rossi tell him to get in touch, perhaps I can be of some help to him too in my way. You are a great help to all of us, Dr. Pereira, said Marta, we of the cause will not forget it. They finished their omelets and Marta said she had to be off. Pereira wished her luck and she slipped nimbly away between the tables. Pereira stayed on and ordered another lemonade. He would have liked to talk all this over with Father António or Dr. Cardoso, but Father António was certainly asleep at that time of night and Dr. Cardoso was away there at Parede. He drank his lemonade and called for the bill. What's the latest news? he asked the waiter when he came to the table. Barbarous goings-on, replied Manuel, barbarous goings-on, Dr. Pereira. Pereira put a hand on his arm. What do you mean by barbarous? he asked. Haven't you heard what's happening in Spain? replied the waiter. No, I haven't, said Pereira. It seems there's some great French writer who's denounced Franco's repression in Spain, said Manuel, and it's created an awful fuss with the Vatican. What's the name of this French writer? asked Pereira. Hmmm, replied Manuel, it's slipped my mind for the moment, he's a writer you'd know for certain, the name's Bernan, Bernadette, something of the sort. Bernanos, exclaimed Pereira, he's called Bernanos! That's it, replied Manuel, that's the name. He's a great Catholic writer, said Pereira with pride, I knew he'd take a stand, he's a man of the highest moral principles. And it occurred to him that perhaps he might publish a couple of chapters of the *Journal d'un curé de campagne*, which had never been translated into Portuguese.

He bade Manuel goodnight and left him a handsome tip. He would have liked to have a talk with Father António, but Father António was assuredly asleep by that time of night, he got up at six every morning to say Mass in the Church of the Mercês, Pereira maintains.

# NINETEEN

The next morning, Pereira maintains, he got up at the crack of dawn and went to pay a call on Father António. He came upon him in his sacristy, just as he was about to disrobe. The sacristy was wonderfully cool, and the walls were covered with religious pictures and ex-votos.

Good morning Father António, said Pereira, here I am at last. Pereira, exclaimed Father António, I haven't seen you for ages, wherever have you been hiding yourself? I've been at Parede, explained Pereira, I spent a week at Parede. At Parede! exclaimed Father António, and what were you doing at Parede? I was at a thalassotherapeutic clinic, replied Pereira, taking seaweed baths and nature cures. Father António asked him to help him remove his stole and said: You certainly get some strange ideas. I've lost nine pounds, said Pereira, and I met a doctor who told me an interesting theory about the soul. Is that why you've come? asked Father António. Partly, admitted Pereira, but I also wanted to talk about other things. Then talk away, said Father António. Well, began Pereira, it's a theory advanced by two French philosophers who are also psychologists, they hold that we do not have a single soul but a confederation of souls guided by a ruling ego, and every now and then this ruling ego changes, so that although we establish a norm it isn't a stable norm, but a variable one. Listen here, Pereira, said Father António, I'm a Franciscan, I'm a simple person, but it seems to me you're becoming a heretic, the human soul is one and indivisible, and it was given us by God. Very well, replied Pereira, but if instead of soul, as the French philosophers have it, we use the word personality, there's an end of heresy, and

I'm convinced that we don't have a single personality, but a lot of personalities living together under the leadership of a ruling ego. That sounds to me a dangerously insidious theory, objected Father António, the personality depends on the soul, and the soul is one and indivisible, what you're saying smacks of heresy. All the same I feel like a different person from what I was a few months ago, said Pereira, I think things I would never have thought and do things I would never have done. Something must have happened in your life, said Father António. I've met two people, said Pereira, a young man and a girl, and maybe meeting them has changed me. It could be, replied Father António, other people influence us, it can happen. I really don't see how they can influence me, said Pereira, they're just two benighted romantics without a future, if anything I ought to influence them, I'm the one who supports them, in fact the young man practically lives at my expense, I do nothing but give him money out of my own pocket, I've taken him on as my assistant but he doesn't write a single article I can publish, I wonder Father António, do you think I ought to make a proper confession? Have you committed any sins of the flesh? asked Father António. The only flesh I know is the flesh I lug around with me, replied Pereira. Then come, Pereira, don't waste my time, because to hear a confession I have to concentrate and I don't want to tire myself out, in a little while I have to visit my sick parishioners, let's by all means talk of this and that and your affairs in general, but not under confession, just as friends.

Father António sat down on a bench in the sacristy and Pereira sat beside him. Listen Father António, said Pereira, I believe in Almighty God, I receive the sacraments, I obey the Ten Commandments and try not to sin, and even if I sometimes don't go to Mass on Sundays it's not for lack of faith but just laziness, I think of myself as a good Catholic and have the teachings of the Church at heart, but at the moment I'm a little confused and also, although I'm a journalist, I'm not well informed about what's going on in the world, and just now I'm very perplexed because it seems there's a lot of argument about the position of the French Catholic writers with regard to the civil war in Spain, I'd like you to put me in the picture, Father António, because you know about things and I'd like to know how to behave so as to avoid falling into heresy. But Pereira, exclaimed Father António, you must be living in another world! Pereira tried to justify himself: Well, the fact is I've been a week in Parede and what's more I haven't bought a foreign paper all summer, and you can't learn much from the Portuguese papers, so the only news I get is café gossip.

Pereira maintains that Father António got to his feet and towered over him with an expression which seemed to him menacingly stern. Pereira, he said, this is a very grave moment and everyone has to make up his own mind, I am a churchman and have to obey my religious superiors, but you are free to make personal decisions, even though you are a Catholic. Then explain me everything, implored Pereira, because I'd like to make my own decisions but I'm not in the know. Father António blew his nose, crossed his hands on his breast and asked: Have you heard of the problem of the Basque clergy? No, I haven't, admitted Pereira. Well, said Father António, it all began with the Basque clergy, because after the bombing of Guernica the Basque clergy, who are considered the most Christian people in Spain, took sides with the Republic. Father António blew his nose as if deeply stirred and continued: In the spring of last year two famous French Catholic writers, François Mauriac and Jacques Maritain, published a manifesto in defense of the Basques. Mauriac! exclaimed Pereira, I said not long ago that we ought to have an obituary ready for Mauriac, he's worth his salt that man, but Monteiro Rossi didn't manage to write one for me. Who is Monteiro Rossi? asked Father António. He's the assistant I've taken on, replied Pereira, but he can't seem to write obituaries for the Catholic writers who have taken up decent political stances. But why do you want an obituary for him, asked Father António, poor Mauriac, let him live, we need him, why d'you want to kill him off? Oh, that's not what I meant at all, said Pereira, I hope he lives to be a hundred, but suppose he were to die suddenly, then there'd be at least one paper in Portugal ready to give him his due, and that paper would be the *Lisboa*, but forgive the interruption Father António, please go on. Well, said Father António, the problem was complicated by the Vatican, which claimed that thousands of the Spanish clergy had been killed by the republicans, that the Basque Catholics were "Red Christians" and deserved to be excommunicated, and sure enough it excommunicated them, and to make matters worse Claudel, the famous Paul Claudel, a Catholic writer himself, wrote an ode, "Aux Martyrs Espagnols" as the preface in verse to a repulsive propaganda leaflet produced by a Spanish nationalist agent in Paris. Claudel! exclaimed Pereira, Paul Claudel? Father António blew his nose yet again. The very same, said he, and how would you define Paul Claudel, Pereira? Well, on the spur of the moment I couldn't presume to say, replied Pereira, he's a Catholic but he's taken a different stance, he has made his decisions. On the spur of the moment you couldn't presume to say, Pereira! exclaimed Father António in turn, well let me tell you that Claudel is a son of a bitch, that's what he is, I'm sorry to utter these words in a holy place because what I'd really like do is shout them from the housetops. What happened next? inquired Pereira. Then, continued Father António, the hierarchy of the Spanish Church, led by Cardinal Gomá, Archbishop of Toledo, decided to send an open letter to all the bishops in the world, you get that Pereira? all the bishops in the world, as if all the bishops in the world were damn Fascists like them, saying that thousands of Christians in Spain had taken up arms of their own accord in defense of the principles of religion. Yes, said Pereira, but what about these Spanish martyrs, all these murdered clergy? Father António was silent for a moment and then said: Martyrs they may possibly be, but the fact remains they were plotting against the Republic, and don't forget that the Republic was constitutional, it had been elected by the people. Franco has made a coup d'état, he's a bandit. And Bernanos, asked Pereira, what's Bernanos got to do with all this? he's a Catholic writer too. He's the only one with first-hand knowledge of Spain, said Father António, from Thirty-Four until last year he was in Spain himself, he has written about the massacres by Franco's troops, the Vatican can't abide him because they know he's a genuine witness. You know, Father António, said Pereira, it has occurred to me to publish a chapter or two of the *Journal d'un curé de campagne* on the culture page of the *Lisboa*, what do you think? I think it's a splendid idea, replied Father António, but I don't know if they'll let you do it, there's no love lost for Bernanos in this country, he's made some pretty harsh comments on the Viriato Battalion, that's the Portuguese military contingent fighting for Franco in Spain, and now you must excuse me Pereira, I must be off to the hospital, my sick parishioners are expecting me.

Pereira got up to take his leave. Good-bye, Father António, said he, I'm sorry to have taken so much of your time, my next visit I'll make a proper confession. You don't need to, replied Father António, first make sure you commit some sin and then come to me, don't make me waste my time for nothing.

Pereira left him and clambered breathlessly up the Rua da Imprensa Nacional. When he reached the church of San Mamede he crossed himself, then dropped onto a bench in the little square, stretched out his legs and settled down to enjoy a breath of fresh air. He would have liked a lemonade, and there was a café only a few steps away. But he resisted the temptation. He simply relaxed in the shade, took off his shoes for a while and let the cool air get to his feet. Then he set off slowly for the office, revolving many memories. Pereira maintains he thought back on his childhood, a childhood spent at Póvoa do Varzim with his grandparents, a happy childhood, or at least one that seemed happy to him, but he has no wish to speak about his childhood because he maintains it has nothing to do with these events and that late August day when summer was on the wane and his mind in such a whirl.

On the stairs he met Celeste who greeted him cheerily and said: Good morning Dr. Pereira, no mail for you this morning or telephone calls either. How d'you mean, telephone calls, exclaimed Pereira, have you been into the office? Of course not, replied the caretaker with an air of triumph, but some workmen from the telephone company came this morning accompanied by an official, they connected your telephone to the porter's lodge, they said it's a a a good idea to have someone to receive the calls when there's no one in the office, and they say I'm a trustworthy person. All too trustworthy as far as that bunch are concerned, Pereira would dearly like to have retorted, but he said nothing of the kind. All he asked was: And what if I have to make a call myself? You have to go through the switchboard, replied Celeste smugly, from now on I am your switchboard, and you have to ask me to obtain the numbers, and I assure you I'd have preferred not to, Dr. Pereira, I work all morning and have to get lunch for four people, because I have four mouths to feed, I do, and apart from the children who get what they get and like it I have a husband who's very demanding, when he gets back from headquarters at two o'clock he's as hungry as a hunter and very demanding. I can tell that from the smell of frying always hanging around on the landing, replied Pereira, and left it at that. He went into the office, took the receiver off the hook and reached into his pocket for the sheet of paper Marta had given him the evening before. It was an article written by hand in blue ink, and at the top was printed ANNIVERSARIES. It read: "Eight years ago, in 1930, the great poet Vladimir Mayakovsky died in Moscow. He shot himself after being disappointed in love. He was the son of a forestry inspector. After joining the Bolshevik party at an early age he was three times arrested and was tortured by the Czarist police. A major propagandist for the Russian revolution, he was a member of the Russian Futurist group, who are politically quite distinct from the Italian Futurists. He toured his country on board a locomotive reciting his revolutionary poems in every village along the way. He aroused great enthusiasm among the people. He was an artist, designer, poet and playwright. His work is not translated into Portuguese, but may be obtained in French from the bookshop in Rua do Ouro in Lisbon. He was a friend of the great Eisenstein, with whom he collaborated on a number of films. He left a vast opus of poetry, prose and drama. In him we celebrate a great democrat and a fervent anti-Czarist."

Pereira, though it was not particularly hot, felt a ring of sweat forming round his collar. He would have liked to toss that article straight in the wastepaper basket, it was just too stupid for words. But instead he opened the file of "Obituaries" and slipped it in. Then he put on his jacket and decided it was time to go home, he maintains.

# TWENTY

That Saturday the translation of Daudet's "The Last Class" was published in the *Lisboa*. The censors had authorized the piece without any fuss and Pereira maintains he thought to himself that one actually could write "*Vive la France!*" after all and that Dr. Cardoso had been wrong about that. Once again Pereira did not sign the translation. This was because he didn't think it proper for the editor of a culture page to sign a translation, he maintains, it would have shown the readers that in fact he wrote the entire page himself, and he didn't like the idea of that. It was a question of pride, he maintains.

Pereira read over the story with a glow of satisfaction, it was ten in the morning, it was Sunday, and because he had gotten up very early he was already in the office, had begun translating the first chapter of the *Journal d'un curé de campagne* by Bernanos and was working away at it vigorously. At that moment the telephone rang. As a rule Pereira took it off the hook, because since it had been connected to the caretaker's switchboard it gave him a creepy feeling to have his calls coming through her, but that morning he'd forgotten. Hello Dr. Pereira, came the voice of Celeste, there's a call for you, you're wanted by the thassalloempyrical clinic in Parede. Thalassotherapeutical, corrected Pereira. Well something of the sort, said the voice of Celeste, do you want to be connected or shall I say you're not in? Put 'em through, said Pereira. He heard the click of a switch and a voice said: Hello, Dr. Cardoso here, I'd like to speak to Dr. Pereira, please. Speaking, replied Pereira, good morning Dr. Cardoso, it's good to hear from you. The pleasure is mine, said Dr. Cardoso, how are you

Dr. Pereira, are you following my diet? I'm doing my best, said Pereira, I'm doing my best but it's not easy. Now Dr. Pereira, said Dr. Cardoso, I'm just off to catch the train for Lisbon, I read the Daudet story yesterday, it's really excellent, I'd like to have a chat about it, how about meeting for lunch? Do you know the Café Orquídea? asked Pereira, it's in Rua Alexandre Herculano, just past the kosher butcher. I know it, said Dr. Cardoso, what time shall we meet, Dr. Pereira? At one, said Pereira, if that suits you. Perfectly, replied Dr. Cardoso, one o'clock it is, I'll see you then. Pereira was certain that Celeste had eavesdropped on every word, but he didn't much care as he hadn't said anything to worry about. He went on translating the first chapter of the Bernanos novel and this time, he maintains, he did take the telephone off the hook. He worked until a quarter to one, then donned his jacket, put his tie in his pocket and sallied forth.

When he entered the Café Orquídea Dr. Cardoso had not yet arrived. Pereira had the table near the fan laid for two and made himself comfortable. He was pretty thirsty, so for an aperitif he ordered a lemonade, but without sugar. When the waiter came with the lemonade Pereira asked him: What's the news, Manuel? Conflicting reports, replied the waiter, it seems that in Spain at the moment there's rather a stalemate, the nationalists have conquered the north but the republicans are getting the better of it in the center of the country, it seems the fifteenth international brigade fought bravely at Saragossa, the center is in republican hands and the Italians fighting for Franco are behaving shamefully. Pereira smiled and asked: Who are you for, Manuel? Sometimes one side and sometimes the other, replied the waiter, because they're both strong, but I don't care for this business of our boys of the Viriato Brigade fighting against the republicans, after all we're a republic ourselves, we kicked out the king in Nineteen Ten, I don't see what reason we have to go fighting against a republic. No more do I, agreed Pereira.

At that moment in came Dr. Cardoso. Pereira had always seen him in a doctor's white coat, and seeing him now in everyday clothes he looked younger, Pereira maintains. Dr. Cardoso was wearing a striped shirt and light-colored jacket and seemed to be feeling the heat. They exchanged a friendly smile, shook hands, and Dr. Cardoso sat down. Tremendous, Dr. Pereira, said he, really tremendous, that really is a beautiful story, I never realized Daudet had such power, I've come to offer my congratulations, but it's a shame you didn't sign the translation, I'd have liked to see your name at the foot of the page. Pereira patiently explained that the reason was humility, or perhaps you could call it pride, because he didn't want the readers to cotton on that the whole page was written by the editor himself, he wanted to give the impression that the paper had other contributors, that it was a proper newspaper, in a word he hadn't signed it for the sake of the *Lisboa*.

They ordered two seafood salads. Pereira would have preferred an omelet *aux fines herbes*, but he didn't dare order one in front of Dr. Cardoso. Perhaps your new ruling ego has scored a point or two, murmured Dr. Cardoso. How do you mean? asked Pereira. I mean that you were capable of writing "*Vive la France!*" said Dr. Cardoso, even though the words were put in someone else's mouth. It did make me feel good, admitted Pereira. And then, with the air of one with all the facts at his fingertips, he went on: Have you heard that the fifteenth international brigade has the upper hand in central Spain? it seems it fought heroically at Saragossa. Don't cherish too many illusions, Dr. Pereira, replied Dr. Cardoso, Mussolini has sent Franco a whole fleet of submarines and the Germans are backing him with their Air Force, the republicans are not going to make it. But they have the Soviets on their side, objected Pereira, the international brigades, people from all over the world have poured down into Spain to give the republicans a hand. I wouldn't cherish too many illusions, repeated Dr. Cardoso, and incidentally I was meaning to tell you that I've reached an agreement with that clinic in Saint-Malo, I'll be leaving in two weeks' time. Don't leave me, Dr. Cardoso! was what Pereira wanted to say, I beg you not to leave me! Instead he said: Don't leave us, Dr. Cardoso, don't leave our people, this country needs people like you. Unfortunately the truth is that it does not need people like me, replied Dr. Cardoso, or at least I don't need it, I think it's better for me to go to France before the disaster strikes. Disaster? exclaimed Pereira, what disaster? I don't know, replied Dr. Cardoso, but I am living in fear of a disaster, a widespread disaster, but I don't want to cause you anxiety, Dr. Pereira, it may be you are working out your new ruling ego and need peace of mind, however I am leaving no matter what, and now tell me about your young people, how are they doing, the youngsters you met who contribute to your paper? Only one of them works for me, replied Pereira, but he has yet to come up with a publishable article, just imagine that yesterday he sent me one on Mayakovsky, talking up that revolutionary Bolshevik, I don't know why I go on giving him good money for unpublishable articles, maybe because he's in trouble, in fact I'm certain of that, and his girl's in trouble too, and I'm the only person they can appeal to. You're helping them, said Dr. Cardoso, I realize that, but helping them less than you'd really like to, perhaps if your new ruling ego comes to the surface you'll do something more, you must excuse me for being frank with you, Dr. Pereira. Look here, Dr. Cardoso, said Pereira, I took on this kid to write anniversaries and advance obituaries and so far he's sent me nothing but raving revolutionary stuff, as if he didn't know what kind of country we're living in, I've always given him money out of my own pocket so as not to burden the paper and because it's better not to involve the editor-in-chief, I've taken him under my wing, I hid his cousin, who seemed to me a dolt and is fighting in the international brigade in Spain, now I'm still sending him money and he's wandering round in Alentejo, what more can I do? You could go and see him, replied Dr. Cardoso simply. Go and see him! exclaimed Pereira, follow him into Alentejo, follow his secret movements, and anyway, where could I go and see him when I don't even know where he's living? His girl will certainly know, said Dr. Cardoso, in fact I'm sure his girl knows but doesn't tell you because she doesn't have complete faith in you, Dr. Pereira, but perhaps you could gain her confidence, be more forthcoming with her, you have a strong superego, Dr. Pereira, and this superego is fighting against your new ruling ego, you are in conflict with yourself in this battle raging in your soul, you must shed your superego, you must allow it to go to its doom like the sloughed-off thing it is. But what would be left of me? quavered Pereira, I am what I am, with my memories, my past life, the memories I have of Coimbra, of my wife, a whole lifetime as a reporter on a great newspaper, what would be left of me? You must work your way through grief, said Dr. Cardoso, it's a Freudian concept, you must forgive me, I am a syncretist so I've drawn ideas from here there and everywhere, but what you need to do is slough off grief, you have to say good-bye to your past life, you need to live in the present, a man cannot live as you do, Dr. Pereira, thinking only of the past. But what about my memories, cried Pereira, all the things that have happened to me? They would be memories and nothing but memories, replied Dr. Cardoso, they would not tyrannize so violently over your present, your life is all backward-looking, for you it's as if you were in Coimbra thirty years ago with your wife still alive, if you go on this way you'll become a sort of fetishist of memories, maybe you'll even start talking to your wife's photograph. Pereira wiped his mouth with his napkin, lowered his voice and said: Dr. Cardoso, I already do. Dr. Cardoso smiled. I saw the picture of your wife in your room at the clinic, he said, and I thought: this man converses mentally with his wife's portrait, he has not yet done his grief-work, that's exactly what I thought, Dr. Pereira. To be perfectly frank it's not that I converse mentally, confessed Pereira, I talk out loud, I tell it everything that happens to me and it's as if the picture answers me. These are fantasies dictated by the superego, said Dr. Cardoso, you should talk to someone real about such things. But I have no one to talk to, confessed Pereira, I live alone, I have a friend who teaches at the University of Coimbra, I went to visit him at the spa at Buçaco and left the very next day because I couldn't stand him, these dons are all of them in favor of the present regime and he's no exception, and then there's my editor-in-chief, but he's on show at all the official functions with his arm stuck out like a javelin, just imagine me talking to him of all people, and then there's Celeste, the caretaker at the office, who's a police spy and is now my switchboard operator into the bargain, and then there's Monteiro Rossi, but he's in hiding. He's the young fellow you met recently, isn't he? asked Dr. Cardoso. Yes, he's my assistant, replied Pereira, the one who writes articles I can't publish. You should seek him out, said Dr. Cardoso, as I said before you should go and seek him out, he's young, he's the future, you badly need young company, even if he does write articles which can't be published in your paper, stop haunting your past and try to drop in on the future. What a splendid way of putting it, said Pereira, to drop in on the future, it would never have occurred to me to put it that way. Pereira ordered a lemonade without sugar and continued: And then there'd be you, Dr. Cardoso, I find it easy to talk to you and would like to talk to you again and again, but you're leaving us, you're leaving me, you're leaving me alone here, and I'll have no one except that photograph of my wife, as you can well understand. Dr. Cardoso drank the coffee which Manuel had brought him. We can talk at Saint-Malo if you'll come and look me up, Dr. Pereira, said Dr.

Cardoso, I'm far from convinced that this is the right country for you, it's too full of memories, try to toss your superego out of the window and make room for your new ruling ego, maybe then we'll be able to meet again and you'll be a new man.

Dr. Cardoso insisted on paying for lunch and Pereira was only too glad to accept, he maintains, because what with those two big banknotes he'd handed over to Marta the evening before his wallet wasn't exactly flush. Dr. Cardoso stood up and said: Good-bye for now, Dr. Pereira, I hope to see you in France or some other country in this great wide world, and don't forget, make room for your new ruling ego, let it come into being, it needs to be born, it needs to assert itself.

Pereira also got to his feet to say good-bye. He watched the other go off and he felt a pang of loss, he maintains, as if that parting were something irremediable. He pondered on the week he had spent at the thalassotherapeutic clinic at Parede, on his conversations with Dr. Cardoso, on his own loneliness. And when Dr. Cardoso passed through the door and disappeared into the street he felt alone, really and truly alone, and it dawned on him that when one is really and truly alone, that is the moment to come to terms with the ruling ego striving to assert itself over one's cohorts of souls. But in spite of this thought he did not feel reassured. On the contrary he felt this deep yearning, for exactly what he cannot presume to say, but it was a profound yearning for a life that was past and for one in the future, Pereira maintains.

# TWENTY-ONE

The next morning, he maintains, Pereira was awakened by the telephone. He was still in the middle of a dream which he seemed to have been dreaming all night, a very long happy dream which he does not think it proper to reveal because it has nothing to do with these events.

Pereira instantly recognized the voice of Senhora Filipa, the editor-in-chief's secretary. Good morning Dr. Pereira, said Filipa in dulcet tones, I'll put you through to the Chief. Pereira rubbed the sleep from his eyes and sat up on the edge of the bed. Good morning Dr. Pereira, said the well-known voice, this is your editor-in-chief speaking. Good morning sir, replied Pereira, did you have a good holiday? Excellent, excellent, replied the editor-in-chief, the spa at Buçaco is truly magnificent, but I think I have already told you that, we have spoken since then if I am not mistaken. Ah, yes, of course, said Pereira, we spoke when the Balzac story came out, I do apologize but I've only just woken up and I haven't got my ideas straight yet. That can happen to any of us, said the editor-in-chief somewhat tartly, and I imagine it can happen even to you, Dr. Pereira. It can indeed, agreed Pereira, it happens mostly first thing in the morning because I have sudden fluctuations of blood pressure. Stabilize them with a little salt, advised the editor-in-chief, a little salt under the tongue will stabilize your blood pressure, but I have not called you to talk about your blood pressure, Dr. Pereira, the fact is that you never come into the head office, that's the problem, you stay shut up in that room in Rua Rodrigo da Fonseca and never come and discuss anything with me, you don't tell me your plans, you do everything on your own.

Forgive me for saying so, sir, said Pereira, but the fact is you gave me *carte blanche*, you said the culture page was my responsibility, I mean you actually instructed me to do everything on my own. That's all very well, continued the editor-in-chief, but don't you think that every now and then you ought to confer with me? It would be a good thing for me too, agreed Pereira, because the fact is I'm all on my own on the culture page, far more than I like, but you told me you didn't want anything to do with the culture page. What about your assistant, asked the editor-in-chief, didn't you tell me you had taken on an assistant? Yes, replied Pereira, but his articles are still somewhat unpolished, and anyway no interesting writer has died, and he's young and asked to go on holiday, I suppose he's off at the beach, I haven't seen him for nearly a month. Fire him, Dr. Pereira, said the editor-in-chief, what are you doing with an assistant who can't write articles and goes off on holiday? Let's give him one more chance, replied Pereira, after all he has to learn the job, he's just an inexperienced youngster, he has to start at the bottom and work up. At that moment the dulcet tones of Senhora Filipa interrupted the conversation. Excuse me sir, but there's a call for you from the Ministry, it seems urgent. Very well, Dr. Pereira, said the editor-in-chief, I'll have a call put through to you in about twenty minutes, meanwhile for goodness' sake wake up properly and dissolve a little salt under your tongue. I'll call you back if you like, said Pereira. No, said the editor-in-chief, I do not wish to be hurried, you will hear from me when I am ready, good-bye.

Pereira got up and had a quick bath. He made coffee and ate a salty biscuit. Then he dressed and went into the hall. The editor-in-chief is calling me back, he told his wife's photograph, it seems to me he's beating around the bush and hasn't yet come to the point, I don't understand what he's going on about but he ought to come to the point, don't you think? His wife's photo smiled its faraway smile and Pereira said: Ah well, never mind, we'll see what it's all about, I have nothing to blame myself for, at least as far as the paper is concerned, I do nothing but translate nineteenth-century French stories.

He sat himself down at the dining room table and thought he might begin an anniversary article on Rilke. But when it came right down to it he had not the slightest wish to write anything at all about Rilke, that snobbish society-haunting dandy could go to the devil, thought Pereira. He set about translating a few sentences from the Bernanos novel, it was more intricate than he had thought, at least at the beginning, and this was only the first chapter, he hadn't yet got into the story. At that moment the telephone rang. Good morning again, Dr. Pereira, said the dulcet tones of Senhora Filipa, I have the Chief on the line for you. Pereira waited a few seconds and then the voice of the editor-in-chief, measured and grave, intoned: Well, Dr. Pereira, where were we? You were telling me that I shut myself up in my office in Rua Rodrigo da Fonseca, sir, said Pereira, but that's the room where I work, where I edit the culture page, at the head office I wouldn't know what to do, I don't know the journalists there, I was a reporter for many years on another paper, but you didn't want to put me in charge of the news desk, you gave me the culture page, with the political journalists I have no contact at all, I don't know what I'd be coming to head office to do. Have you gotten that off your chest, Dr. Pereira? asked the editor-in-chief. I'm sorry sir, said Pereira, I didn't wish to get anything off my chest, I just wanted to explain my position. Very well, said the editor-in-chief, but now I want to ask you a simple question, why do you never feel it necessary to come and talk things over with your Chief? Because you told me that culture is not up your street, sir, replied Pereira. Look here Dr. Pereira, said the editor-in-chief, I don't know if you are hard of hearing or just don't want to understand, but the fact is I am calling you in to the office, do you get that? you should be the one to ask for an occasional talk with me, but at this point, seeing that you are so slow on the uptake it is I who am asking for a talk with you. I am at your disposal, said Pereira, completely at your disposal. Good, said the editor-in-chief, then come to my office at five o'clock this evening, so good-bye until then, Dr. Pereira.

Pereira became aware that he was sweating slightly. His shirt was wet under the armpits, so he changed it. He contemplated going to his office and waiting till five o'clock. Then he told himself that there was nothing to do in the office, he would be forced to see Celeste and take the telephone off the hook, it was better to stay at home. He went back to the dining room table and got on with his translation of Bernanos. It certainly was an intricate novel, and also slow-moving, he wondered what the readers of the *Lisboa* would think when they read the first chapter. Nevertheless he pushed ahead and translated two pages. At lunchtime he thought of cooking himself something, but there was practically nothing in the cupboard. He thought the best thing to do was have a late bite of lunch at the Café Orquídea, he maintains, and then go on to the main office. He put on his light summer suit and black tie and left the house. He took the tram to Terreiro do Paço and changed there for Rua Alexandre Herculano. By the time he reached the Café Orquídea it was nearly three and Manuel was clearing the tables. Come on in Dr. Pereira, said the waiter cordially, for you there's always a little something, I take it you haven't eaten yet, it's a hard life is a journalist's. You're right there, replied Pereira, especially for journalists who don't know anything because no one ever knows anything in this country, what's the news? It seems some English ships have been bombed off Barcelona, replied Manuel, and a French passenger ship was tracked all the way to the Dardanelles, it's the Italian submarines, they're very hot on submarines are the Italians, it's their specialty. Pereira ordered a lemonade without sugar and an omelet *aux fines herbes*. He took a seat near the fan, but that day the fan was off. We've switched it off, said Manuel, summer's over, didn't you hear the storm last night? No I didn't, replied Pereira, I never stirred all night, but I personally still find it pretty hot. Manuel switched on the fan and brought him a lemonade. And a drop of wine, Dr. Pereira, when will you give me the pleasure of serving you a drop of wine? Wine is bad for my heart, replied Pereira, have you got a morning paper? Manuel brought him a paper. The main headline read: "Sand Carvings on Carcavelos Beach. Minister of Secretariado Nacional de Propaganda Opens Exhibition of Youthful Artists." Further down the page was a large photograph of the works of the young beach artists, with a display of mermaids, boats, ships, whales and so forth. Pereira turned the page. Inside he read: "Gallant Resistance of Portuguese Contingent in Spain." The subhead ran: "Our soldiers distinguish themselves in another battle with long-range support from Italian submarines." Pereira did not feel inclined to read the article and laid the newspaper on a chair. He finished his omelet and had another lemonade without sugar. Then he paid the bill, got up, put on his discarded jacket and set off on foot to the head office of the *Lisboa*. When he got there it was still only a quarter to five. Pereira went to a café, he maintains, and ordered an aqua vitae. It was sure to be bad for his heart, but he thought: What the hell. Then he climbed the stairs of the old building where the *Lisboa* had its offices and said good afternoon to Senhora Filipa. I'll go and announce you, said Senhora Filipa. Don't worry, said Pereira, I'll see myself in, it's exactly five o'clock and my appointment is at five. He knocked at the door and heard the editor-in-chief say come in. Pereira buttoned his jacket and entered. The editor-in-chief was looking tanned, very tanned and fit, he had evidently taken plenty of sun in the gardens at the spa. Here I am sir, said Pereira, at your service, tell me all.

That's soon done, Pereira, said the editor-in-chief, it's that you haven't been to see me for more than a month. We met at the spa, said Pereira, and you seemed satisfied with the way things were going. Holidays are holidays, snapped the editor-in-chief, we are not here to talk about holidays. Pereira seated himself facing the desk. The editor-in-chief picked up a pencil and started rolling it this way and that on the desktop. Look here, Pereira, said the editor-in-chief, we have not known each other all that long, only since this newspaper was founded, but I would like to address you in informal fashion if I may. As you wish, replied Pereira. I know you are an experienced journalist, resumed the editor-in-chief, you worked for thirty years as a reporter, you know life and I'm sure you will understand what I am going to say. I'll do my level best, promised Pereira. Well then, said the editor-in-chief, I really didn't expect this latest thing. What latest thing? asked Pereira. That panegyric on France, said the editor-in-chief, has caused a lot of offense in high places. What panegyric on France? asked Pereira, totally bewildered. Come now Pereira! exclaimed the editor-in-chief, you published a story by Alphonse Daudet about the Franco-Prussian War which ended with the phrase: "*Vive la France!*" But it's a nineteenth-century story, replied Pereira. A nineteenth-century story it may be, continued the editor-in-chief, but it is nonetheless concerned with a war against Germany, and you cannot be ignorant of the fact, Pereira, that Germany is our ally. Our government has made no alliances, retorted Pereira, at least not officially. Come off it Pereira, said the editor-in-chief, use your head. If there are no alliances there are at least sympathies, strong sympathies, we think along the same lines as Germany does, in home as in foreign policy, and we are supporting the Spanish nationalists just as the Germans are. But the censors raised no objections, said Pereira stoutly, they passed the story without any trouble. The censors are a bunch of illiterate boobies, said the editor-in-chief, the chief censor is an intelligent man, a friend of mine, but he cannot personally read the proofs of every newspaper in Portugal, the others are just officials, garden-variety policemen paid not to let through subversive words such as socialism or communism, they could scarcely be expected to understand a story by Daudet ending with the words "*Vive la France!*" it is we who must be vigilant, we who must be cautious, we journalists who are versed in history and culture, we have to keep a watchful eye on ourselves. There's a watchful eye on me all right, rejoined Pereira, he maintains, there's someone actually keeping me under surveillance. Explain yourself, Pereira, said the editor-in-chief, what do you mean by that? I mean that my office now has a switchboard, said Pereira, I no longer get my telephone calls direct, they all go through Celeste, the caretaker. It's that way in all newspaper offices, replied the editor-in-chief, if you are out there is always someone to receive your calls and take a message. All right, said Pereira, but the caretaker is a police informer, I'm sure of it. Come off it Pereira, said the editor-in-chief, the police are there to protect us, they watch while we sleep, you ought to be grateful to them. I am grateful to no one and nothing, sir, except my professional ability and the memory of my wife. One must always be grateful for happy memories, murmured the editor-in-chief unctuously, but you, Pereira, must no longer publish the culture page without letting me see it first, this I insist on. But I told you beforehand that it was a patriotic story, argued Pereira, and you encouraged me by saying that in times like these we all need patriotism. The editor-in-chief lit a cigarette and scratched his head. *Portuguese* patriotism, I don't know if you follow me Pereira, we need *Portuguese* patriotism, and you do nothing but publish French stories and the French are not congenial to us, if you follow me, however the fact is this, what our readers need is a good Portuguese cultural page, there are dozens of Portuguese writers to choose from, even nineteenth-century writers, for the next issue choose a story by Eça da Queiros, who really knew his Portugal, or Camilo Castelo Branco, who was truly romantic and led an adventurous life, always in and out of love and prison, the *Lisboa* is not a foreign-oriented newspaper, you need to rediscover your roots, Pereira, to return to your native sod, in the words of the critic Borrapotas. Never heard of him, said Pereira. He is a critic and a nationalist, explained the editor-in-chief, who writes for a rival paper and holds the view that Portuguese writers must return to their native sod. I have never left my native sod, said Pereira, I am planted in it like a stake. Quite, quite, conceded the editor-in-chief, but I wish you to consult me before any new undertaking, I don't know if you grasp my point. I grasp it perfectly, said Pereira, undoing the top button of his jacket. Good, concluded the editor-in-chief, then I think that is all we have to discuss, I would like there to be good relations between us. Quite, echoed Pereira, and took his leave.

When he reached the street a strong wind was swaying the treetops. Pereira started out on foot, then stopped to wait for a cruising taxi. At first he thought he would have some supper at the Café Orquídea, then changed his mind and came to the conclusion that it would be wiser to have a café au lait at home. But unfortunately no taxis came cruising past, he had to wait a good half hour, he maintains.

# TWENTY-TWO

Next day Pereira stayed at home, he maintains. He got up late, breakfasted, and put aside the novel by Bernanos, as now there was no chance it would be published in the *Lisboa*. He hunted through his bookshelves and found the complete works of Camilo Castelo Branco. He picked out a story at random and started to read. He found it oppressively dull, it had none of the lightness and irony of the French writers, it was a gloomy, nostalgic tale full of problems and fraught with tragedy. Pereira soon tired of it. He had an urge to talk to his wife's photograph, but he postponed the conversation until later. He made himself an omelet without *fines herbes*, ate every scrap of it and went to take a nap. He fell asleep at once and had a beautiful dream. Then he got up, settled himself in an armchair and gazed out of the window. From the windows of his flat he had a view of the palm trees in front of the barracks over the way and every so often he heard a bugle call. Pereira couldn't decipher the bugle calls because he had never done military service, for him they were nonsense messages. He just gazed at the palm fronds tossing in the wind and thought of his childhood. He spent a large part of the afternoon like this, thinking of his childhood, but it is something Pereira has no wish to talk about, as it has nothing to do with these events, he maintains.

At about four o'clock he heard the doorbell ring. Pereira tried to shake off his drowsiness but did not stir. He found it odd that anyone should be ringing the bell, he thought vaguely it might be Piedade back from Setúbal, perhaps her sister had been operated on sooner than expected. The bell rang again, insistently, twice, two long peals. Pereira got up and pulled a lever to unlatch the street door. He stayed on the landing, heard the door very quietly close and footsteps hastening up the staircase. When the figure reached the landing Pereira couldn't make out who it was, the stairwell was so dark and his sight not as good as it used to be.

Hello Dr. Pereira, said a voice which Pereira did recognize, hello it's me, may I come in? It was Monteiro Rossi. Pereira let him in and closed the door at once. Monteiro Rossi stopped in the hall, he was carrying a small bag and wearing a short-sleeved shirt. Forgive me, Dr. Pereira, said Monteiro Rossi, later on I'll explain everything, is there anyone in the building? The caretaker is at Setúbal, said Pereira, the tenants on the floor above have left the flat empty, they've moved to Oporto. Do you think anyone can have seen me? panted Monteiro Rossi. He was sweating and stammering slightly. I wouldn't think so, said Pereira, but what are you doing here, where have you come from? I'll explain everything later, Dr. Pereira, said Monteiro Rossi, for the moment what I need is a shower and a clean shirt, I'm dead beat. Pereira showed him to the bathroom and gave him a clean shirt, his own khaki shirt. It'll be on the big side, he said, but never mind. While Monteiro Rossi was in the bathroom Pereira went and stood in the hall looking at his wife's photograph. He would have liked to tell it lots of things, he maintains, that Monteiro Rossi had suddenly turned up, for example, and other things besides. Instead he said nothing, he postponed the conversation until later and returned to the living room. Monteiro Rossi came in absolutely swamped in Pereira's outsize shirt. Thank you Dr. Pereira, he said, I'm dead beat, there's lots I want to tell you but I'm absolutely dead beat, maybe what I need is a nap. Pereira took him into the bedroom and spread a cotton blanket over the sheets. Lie down here, he said, and take off your shoes, don't go to sleep with shoes on because your body won't relax, and don't worry, I'll wake you later.

Monteiro Rossi lay down and Pereira closed the door and returned to the living room. He pushed aside the stories of Camilo Castelo Branco, reopened Bernanos and set about translating the rest of the chapter. If he couldn't publish it in the *Lisboa* well never mind, he thought, maybe he could publish it in book form, at least the Portuguese would then have one good book to read, a serious, moral book, one that dealt with fundamental problems, a book that would do a power of good to the consciences of its readers, thought Pereira.

At eight o'clock Monteiro Rossi was still sleeping. Pereira went into the kitchen, beat up four eggs, added a spoonful of Dijon mustard and a pinch each of oregano and marjoram. He wanted to make a good omelet *aux fines herbes*, very likely Monteiro Rossi was as hungry as a hunter, he thought. He laid the table for two, spreading out a white cloth and using the plates made in Caldas da Rainha which Silva had given him for a wedding present and fixing candles in the two candlesticks. Then he went to wake Monteiro Rossi, but he crept in on tiptoe because he really felt it was a shame to wake him. The young man was sprawled on the bed with one arm flung out. Pereira called his name, but Monteiro Rossi didn't stir. So Pereira shook him by the arm and said: Monteiro Rossi, it's time for supper, if you go on sleeping now you won't sleep tonight, you'd better come and have a bite to eat. Monteiro Rossi leapt from the bed, obviously terrified. No need to be nervous, Pereira said, it's Dr. Pereira, you're quite safe here. They went into the dining room and Pereira lit the candles. While he was cooking the omelet he offered Monteiro Rossi some tinned paté which he'd discovered in the cupboard, and from the kitchen he called: What's been going on then, Monteiro Rossi? Thank you, was Monteiro Rossi's reply, thank you for your hospitality Dr. Pereira, and thanks also for the money you sent me, Marta got it through to me. Pereira brought the omelet to the table and tied his napkin round his neck. Well then, Monteiro Rossi, he said, what's going on? Monteiro Rossi fell on the food as though he hadn't eaten for a week. Take it easy, you'll choke, said Pereira, eat more slowly, and anyway there's cheese to follow, and now tell me everything. Monteiro Rossi swallowed his mouthful and said: My cousin has been arrested. Where? asked Pereira, at the hotel I found for him? No, no, replied Monteiro Rossi, he was arrested in Alentejo while trying to recruit Alentejans, I only escaped by a miracle. And what now? asked Pereira. Now I'm on the run, Dr. Pereira, replied Monteiro Rossi, I suppose they're hunting for me all over Portugal, I caught a bus yesterday evening and got as far as Barreiro, then I took a ferry, and from Cais de Sodré I've slogged it on foot because I didn't have the money for the fare. Does anyone know you're here? asked Pereira. No one at all, replied Monteiro Rossi, not even Marta, in fact I want to get in touch with her, I want at least Marta to know I'm in a safe place, because you won't turn me out, will you Dr. Pereira? You can stay as long as you like, replied Pereira, or at least until mid-September when Piedade gets back, Piedade is the caretaker here and also my daily, she's a trustworthy woman but she's a caretaker, and caretakers natter to other caretakers, your presence would not pass unobserved. Okay, said Monteiro Rossi, between now and the fifteenth of September I'll surely find somewhere else to go, maybe I'll get on to Marta at once. Look here Monteiro Rossi, said Pereira, let Marta be for now, as long as you're in my house don't get in touch with anyone, just stay put and rest. And how are things going for you, Dr. Pereira, asked Monteiro Rossi, still busy with obituaries and anniversaries? Partly, replied Pereira, however the articles you have written are all unpublishable, I've put them in a file in the office, I don't know why I don't throw them away. It's time I owned up to something, murmured Monteiro Rossi, I'm sorry I've taken so long about it, but those articles are not all my own work. How do you mean? asked Pereira. Well Dr. Pereira, the truth is that Marta gave me a lot of help with them, she wrote them partly herself, the basic ideas are hers. How extremely improper, said Pereira. Oh, replied Monteiro Rossi, I wouldn't go that far, but Dr. Pereira have you heard the Spanish nationalist slogan? their slogan is *Viva la muerte!* and I can't write about death, what I love is life, Dr. Pereira, and I'd never have managed to write obituaries on my own, to talk about death, I'm really not able to talk about it. All in all I'm with you there, said Pereira, so he maintains, I can't stand it any longer myself.

Darkness had fallen and the candles shed a wan light. I don't know why I'm doing all this for you Monteiro Rossi, said Pereira. Perhaps it's because you're a decent person, replied Monteiro Rossi. That's too simple, retorted Pereira, the world is full of decent people but they don't go looking for trouble. Then I don't know, said Monteiro Rossi, I really can't imagine. The real problem is that I don't know either, said Pereira, until a few days ago I kept on asking myself, but maybe it's better for me to stop asking. He brought cherries in maraschino to the table and Monteiro Rossi helped himself to a whole glassful. Pereira took only one cherry and a drop of juice, because he was afraid of ruining his diet.

But tell me all about it, said Pereira, what have you been up to all this time in Alentejo? We covered the whole region, replied Monteiro Rossi, stopping in the safe places, the places where there's most turbulence. Excuse me, put in Pereira, but your cousin scarcely seems a suitable person, I only saw him the once but he seemed to me a little ill-equipped, I'd even say rather slow-witted, and on top of that he doesn't even speak Portuguese. True, said Monteiro Rossi, but in civilian life he's a printer, he's good at handling documents, there's no one like him for forging a passport. Then he might have done a better job on his own, said Pereira, he had an Argentine passport you could see was a fake from a mile off. He didn't make that one himself, replied Monteiro Rossi, they gave it him in Spain. And then what? asked Pereira. Well, replied Monteiro Rossi, we found a safe printer's in Portalegre and my cousin got to work, we did a first-class job, my cousin made up a whole bunch of passports, a lot of them we managed to distribute but some are left over because we didn't have time. Monteiro Rossi picked up his bag from an armchair and reached into it. Here's what I've got left over, he said. And he placed a bundle of passports on the table, there must have been a couple of dozen of them. My dear Monteiro Rossi you are mad, said Pereira, you go around with those things in your bag as if they were candy, if they find you with these documents you'll be in big trouble.

Pereira picked up the passports and said: I'll see to hiding these. He first thought of putting them in a drawer, but that didn't seem safe enough. Then he went into the hall and slid them into the bookshelves right behind his wife's photograph. Please excuse me, said he, addressing the picture, but no one will come looking here, it's the safest place in the whole house. Then he went back to the living room and said: Time's getting on, maybe we'd better go to bed. I've got to get in touch with Marta, said Monteiro Rossi, she'll be worried, she doesn't know what's become of me, she might think they've arrested me as well. Look here Monteiro Rossi, said Pereira, tomorrow I'll call Marta myself, but from a public telephone, for this evening the best thing for you is to stop worrying and get to bed, jot me down the number on this pad. I'll give you two numbers, said Monteiro Rossi, if she doesn't answer at one she'll certainly be at the other, and if she doesn't answer in person ask to speak to Lise Delaunay, that's what she calls herself now. I know, admitted Pereira, I met her a few days ago, that girl has gotten as thin as a rake, she's unrecognizable, this way of life is no good for her, Monteiro Rossi, she's ruining her health, and now off to bed.

Pereira snuffed out the candles and asked himself why he had gotten mixed up in this, why shelter Monteiro Rossi and call Marta and leave coded messages, why meddle with things that didn't concern him? Was it perhaps that Marta had gotten so thin that her shoulder blades stuck out like the wings of a plucked chicken? Was it that Monteiro Rossi had no mother or father to shelter him? Was it his visit to Parede and Dr. Cardoso explaining his theory of the confederation of souls? Pereira did not know, and even today he could not presume to say. He wanted to get to bed because next morning he intended to be up early and make careful arrangements for the day, but before doing so he went into the hall for a brief glance at his wife's photograph. He said not a word to it, just gave it an affectionate wave of the hand, he maintains.

# TWENTY-THREE

That late August morning Pereira woke at eight, he maintains. Several times during the night he had woken and heard rain pelting down on the palm trees of the barracks over the way. He doesn't remember dreaming, he'd slept fitfully with a few dreams now and then, presumably, but he doesn't remember them. Monteiro Rossi was asleep on the living room sofa, wearing a pair of pajamas so huge on him they could practically have served as sheets. He was sleeping all bunched up, as if he was freezing cold, and Pereira spread a rug over him, very gently so as not to wake him. He moved gingerly round the flat for fear of making a noise, brewed himself some coffee, then set off to get supplies at the grocer's on the corner. He bought four tins of sardines, a dozen eggs, tomatoes, a melon, a loaf, and eight ready-made salt cod fishcakes. Then he spotted, hanging on a hook, a small smoked ham sprinkled with paprika, and he bought that too. So you've decided to stock up your larder, Dr. Pereira, commented the grocer. Well yes, replied Pereira, my daily won't be back until mid-September, she's with her sister at Setúbal, I have to look after myself and I can't go shopping every morning. If you want a capable woman to come in and do for you I can recommend one, said the grocer, she lives a little up the hill, near La Graça, she's got a small child and her husband has left her, she's a reliable person. No, thank you all the same, Senhor Francisco, replied Pereira, it's better not, I don't know how Piedade would take it, there's a lot of jealousy between these dailies and she might feel ousted, maybe over the winter it might be an idea, but just now I'd better wait until Piedade gets back.

Pereira went home and put his purchases in the ice chest. Monteiro Rossi was still asleep. Pereira left him a note: "There's ham and eggs or fishcakes to heat up, you heat them in a frying pan with only a little oil, otherwise they go to a mush, have a good lunch and don't worry, I'll be back late afternoon, I'll speak to Marta, see you later, Pereira."

He left the house and went to the office. There he found Celeste in her cubbyhole busying herself with a calendar. Good morning Celeste, said Pereira, anything for me? No telephone calls and no mail, replied Celeste. Pereira felt relieved, all the better that no one had tried to get in touch with him. He went up to the office and took the telephone off the hook, then reached for the story by Camilo Castelo Branco and prepared it for the press. At about ten o'clock he called the head office and was answered by the dulcet tones of Senhora Filipa. This is Dr. Pereira, said Pereira, I would like to speak to the editor-in-chief. Filipa put through the call and the voice of the editor-in-chief said: Hello. This is Dr. Pereira, said Pereira, I just wanted to keep in touch, sir. You do well, said the editor-in-chief, because I tried to get you yesterday but you were not in the office. I wasn't feeling too well yesterday, lied Pereira, I stayed at home because my heart was playing me up. I quite understand, Dr. Pereira, said the editor-in-chief, however I would like to know what your intentions are for the forthcoming culture pages. I am publishing a story by Camilo Castelo Branco, replied Pereira, as you suggested yourself sir, a nineteenth-century Portuguese author should fit the bill, don't you think? Very much so, replied the editor-in-chief, but I think you should also continue the anniversaries feature. I had thought of doing Rilke, said Pereira, but I left it because I wanted your approval. Rilke, said the editor-in-chief, the name does seem vaguely familiar. Rainer Maria Rilke, explained Pereira, born in Czechoslovakia but to all intents and purposes an Austrian poet, he wrote in German and died in Nineteen Twenty-

Six. Look here Pereira, said the editor-in-chief, as I told you before the *Lisboa* is becoming much too foreign-oriented, why not do an anniversary feature on one of our Portuguese poets, why not do our great Camoens? Camoens? replied Pereira, but Camoens died in Fifteen Eighty, nearly four hundred years ago. True, said the editor-in-chief, but he is always topical, and haven't you heard that António Ferro, Director of the Secretariado Nacional de Propaganda, in short the Minister of Culture, has had the brilliant idea of celebrating Camoens Day on Portuguese Race Celebration Day, so that we shall celebrate our great epic poet and the Portuguese Race on one and the same day, and an anniversary feature will be just the thing. But sir, Camoens Day is the tenth of June, objected Pereira, what sense does it make to celebrate Camoens Day at the end of August? Ha! but on the tenth of June we didn't yet have our culture page, argued the editor-in-chief, and you can point out as much in your article, and then you can always simply celebrate Camoens, who is our great national poet, and merely make some reference to Race Celebration Day, the least reference would be enough for our readers to get the message. Please bear with me sir, replied Pereira with some compunction, but I feel I must tell you that originally we were Lusitanians, and then came the Romans and the Celts, and then came the Arabs, so what sort of race are we Portuguese in a position to celebrate? The Portuguese Race, replied the editor-in-chief, and I am sorry to say, Pereira, that I don't like the tone of your objection, we are Portuguese, we discovered the world, we achieved the greatest feats of navigation the world over, and when we did this, in the sixteenth century, we were already Portuguese, that is what we are and that is what you are to celebrate, Pereira. The editor-in-chief paused and then continued: Pereira, last time we talked I addressed you informally and I don't know why I have gone back to using the formalities. Do as you please sir, replied Pereira, perhaps it's the telephone that has that effect. You may be right, said the editor-in-chief, however please pay attention to what I say, Pereira, I want the *Lisboa* to be an ultra-Portuguese paper, not least in its culture page, and if you don't want to do an anniversary feature for Portuguese Race Celebration Day you must at least do one for Camoens, that will be better than nothing.

Pereira said: Very well, good-bye, and hung up. António Ferro, he thought, that frightful António Ferro, the worst of it was he was a shrewd, intelligent man, and just to think he'd been a friend of Fernando Pessoa's, ah well, concluded Pereira, it must be admitted that even Pessoa picked himself some pretty strange friends. Pereira then had a shot at an anniversary feature on Camoens and stuck at it until half past twelve. He then threw them all in the wastepaper basket. The devil take Camoens as well, he thought, that great bard who sang the heroism of the Portuguese Race, ha ha, some heroism, thought Pereira. He put on his jacket and left the office for the Café Orquídea. There he took his place at the usual table. Manuel came bustling up and Pereira ordered a seafood salad. He ate slowly, very slowly, then went to the telephone. He fished out the scrap of paper with the numbers Monteiro Rossi had given him. The first number rang for a long time but no one answered. He called it again, he had misdialed so often in the past. The number rang for a long time but no one answered. Then he tried the other number. A woman's voice came on the line. Hello, said Pereira, I would like to speak to Senhora Delaunay. I don't know anyone of that name, replied the woman's voice cagily. Good afternoon, repeated Pereira, I'm looking for Senhora Delaunay. Excuse me, but who is calling? asked the voice. Listen madam, said Pereira, I have an urgent message for Lise Delaunay, would you kindly put her on. There is no one here by the name of Lise, said the voice, I think you must have dialed a wrong number, who gave you this number may I ask? It doesn't matter, replied Pereira, but if I can't speak to Lise at least put me on to Marta. Marta? said the woman in apparent bewilderment, Marta who? there are so many Martas in this world. Pereira realized he didn't know Marta's surname so he simply said: Marta is a thin girl with blonde hair who also answers to the name of Lise Delaunay, I am a friend and have an important message for her. I'm sorry, said the woman but there's no Marta here and no Lise either, good afternoon. The telephone went click and Pereira was left with the receiver in his hand. He hung up and returned to his table. What can I bring you? asked Manuel, bustling up. Pereira ordered a lemonade with sugar, then asked: Any news of interest? I'll be finding out at eight o'clock this evening, said Manuel, I have a friend who gets the BBC from London, I'll tell you everything tomorrow if you like.

Pereira drank his lemonade and paid the bill. He left and went back to his office. He found Celeste in her cubbyhole still poring over the calendar. Anything new? asked Pereira. There was a phone call for you, said Celeste, it was a woman but she wasn't too keen on telling her business. Did she leave a name? asked Pereira. It was a foreign-sounding name, replied Celeste, but it's slipped my mind. Why didn't you write it down? said Pereira reproachfully, you're supposed to work the switchboard, Celeste, you're supposed to take messages. I have enough trouble writing Portuguese, replied Celeste, I can do without foreign names, it was a complicated name. Pereira's heart missed a beat and he asked: And what did this person want, Celeste, what did she say? She said she'd gotten a message for you and she was looking for a Senhor Rossi, what an odd name, and I said there was no one here by the name of Rossi, this was the editorial office of the culture page of the *Lisboa*, so I called the head office because I thought I'd find you there, I wanted to inform you, but you weren't there so I left a message that you were wanted by some foreign lady, a certain Lise, so there! I've remembered it. You told them at the head office that someone was looking for this Senhor Rossi? asked Pereira. No, Dr. Pereira, replied Celeste with a sly wink, I didn't tell them that, I didn't see the point, I just said that this Lise was looking for you, so don't you worry Dr. Pereira, if they want you they'll find you. Pereira glanced at his watch. It was four o'clock, he decided not to go upstairs but said: Listen Celeste, I'm going home because I don't feel too well, if anyone telephones ask them to call me at home, maybe I won't come to the office tomorrow so please take in my mail.

When he got home it was nearly seven. He had dawdled for quite a while at Terreiro do Paço, sitting on a bench and watching the ferries leaving for the other side of the Tagus. It was lovely, that early evening hour, and Pereira felt like making the most of it. He lit a cigar and inhaled deeply. While he was sitting there a tramp came and sat down by him, he had a mouth organ and played him some old Coimbra songs dear to his heart.

When Pereira entered the flat he couldn't find Monteiro Rossi at once and this gave him quite a fright, he maintains. But Monteiro Rossi was in the bathroom doing his ablutions. I'm having a shave, Dr. Pereira, Monteiro Rossi called out, I'll be with you in five minutes. Pereira took off his jacket and laid the table. He used the plates from Caldas da Rainha, as on the night before, and on the table he placed two fresh candles bought that morning. Then he went into the kitchen and wondered what he should make for supper. For some reason it occurred to him to try to make an Italian dish, even though he knew nothing about Italian cooking. He thought he'd invent a dish, he maintains. He carved a thick slice of ham and chopped it into small cubes, then beat up two eggs, stirred in plenty of grated cheese and tipped in the ham, added oregano and marjoram, mixed everything together thoroughly and then put on a pan of water to boil for the pasta. There'd been some spaghetti in the cupboard for quite some time, and when the water boiled he dumped it in. Monteiro Rossi entered looking as fresh as a rose, Pereira's khaki shirt enveloping him like a sheet. I thought I'd make an Italian dish, said Pereira, I don't know if it's really Italian, perhaps it's just an invention but at least it's spaghetti. What a treat, said Monteiro Rossi, I haven't had spaghetti for ages. Pereira lit the candles and dished up. I tried to call Marta, he said, but at the first number there was no answer and the second number was answered by a woman who pretended to be slow on the uptake, I even said I wanted to speak to Marta but it was no use, then when I got to my office the caretaker told me that someone had called me, it was probably Marta looking for you, perhaps rather rash of her, in any case someone now knows I'm in touch with you, I'm afraid this will cause problems. What am I to do? asked Monteiro Rossi. If you've got anywhere safer you'd better go there, replied Pereira, otherwise stay here and we'll wait and see. He fetched the maraschino cherries and took one without any juice. Monteiro Rossi filled his glass. At that moment came knocking at the door. Determined blows fit to break the door down. Pereira wondered how they had managed to get in at the street door, and for a second or two was stricken dumb. The knocking came again, more furious still. Who's there? called Pereira getting to his feet, what do you want? Open up, police, open up or we'll shoot the door down! Monteiro Rossi dashed into the next room, all he managed to blurt out was: The passports, Dr. Pereira, hide the passports. They're already safe, Pereira assured him, and made for the hall to open the door. As he passed his wife's photograph he cast a glance of complicity at that faraway smile. Then he opened the door, he maintains.

# TWENTY-FOUR

Pereira maintains there were three of them, in civilian clothes, pistols in their fists. The first to enter was a seedy little runt with a mustache and brown goatee. Political police, announced the seedy runt with an air of authority, we have orders to search this flat, we're looking for someone. Let me see your identity cards, demanded Pereira stoutly. The seedy runt turned to his companions, two dark-suited thugs, and said: You hear that, boys, what do you think of it? One of the pair pointed his pistol straight at Pereira's mouth and hissed: How's this for identification, fatty? Come come, boys, said the seedy runt, I won't have you treat Dr. Pereira that way, he's a leading journalist, he writes for a respectable newspaper, perhaps a shade too Catholic, I won't deny that, but with the right political alignment, and now Dr. Pereira, stop wasting our time, we haven't come for a cozy chat and wasting time isn't our strong point, anyway we know you're not involved, you're a worthy person, you just didn't know who you were dealing with, you went and placed your confidence in a shady character, but I don't want to get you into trouble, just let's get on with our work. I am the editor of the culture page of the *Lisboa*, spluttered Pereira, I want to speak to someone, I want to telephone to my editor-in-chief, does he know you're here at my house? Come off it, Dr. Pereira, replied the seedy runt in mellifluous tones, do you imagine that before we carry out police operations we inform your editor-in-chief, what can you be thinking? But you're not the police, insisted Pereira, you're not official, you're not in uniform, you have no authority to enter my home. The seedy runt smirked at the two thugs over his shoulder and said: The master of the house is recalcitrant, boys, I wonder how we can make him see reason. The man covering Pereira with his pistol struck him with a backhand so hard that it sent him reeling. Now now Fonseca, that won't do, said the seedy runt, you mustn't mistreat Dr. Pereira, otherwise you'll scare him out of his wits, he's a delicate fellow in spite of being so big and fat, he's in the culture business, he's an intellectual, Dr. Pereira must be persuaded gently else he'll piss in his pants. The thug called Fonseca lashed out with another back-handed blow and Pereira staggered again, he maintains. Fonseca, said the seedy runt with another smirk, you're a little too rough, I'll have to keep my eye on you, buddy, or you'll spoil all my good work. Then he turned to Pereira and said: Dr. Pereira, as I was saying we've got nothing against you, we've only come to teach a little lesson to a young man who's here in your flat, a person who requires a little lesson because he doesn't know the true values of his country, he's lost touch with them, poor kid, and we're here to help him find them again. Pereira rubbed his cheek and mumbled: There's no one here. The seedy runt cast a glance around the place and said: Careful now Dr. Pereira, don't make things hard for us, this young man's your guest and we only want to ask him a few questions, it's only a matter of a brief interrogation to see that he regains his sense of patriotism, that's all we want to do, that's all we've come for. Then let me call the police, insisted Pereira, let them come and take him to headquarters, that's where they carry out interrogations, not in people's homes. Come now, Dr. Pereira, said the seedy runt with his ghost of a smirk, you're not being the least bit cooperative, your place is ideal for a private interrogation like ours, your caretaker is away, your neighbors have moved to Oporto, it's a nice quiet evening and this building is perfect, so much more discreet than a police station, don't you think?

He flicked his fingers at the thug he'd called Fonseca, who shoved Pereira roughly into the dining room. The intruders took a look around but there was no one there, only the table laid for dinner and the remains of the meal. An intimate little dinner, Dr. Pereira, said the seedy runt, I see you've been having an intimate little dinner with candles and all, how romantic. Pereira made no answer. See here Dr. Pereira, said the seedy runt in mellifluous tones, you're a widower and you don't go with women, as you see I know everything about you, it's not that you like young men now, is it? Pereira passed a hand across his cheek again and said: You are the last word in infamy, this whole thing is infamous. Come now Dr. Pereira, continued the seedy runt, a man is but a man as you know very well yourself, and if a man comes across a nice blond youngster with a pretty bit of ass on him it's more than understandable. Then, suddenly spitting out the words: Must we turn the place upside down or would you care to collaborate? He's in there, said Pereira, in one of those rooms through there. The seedy runt gave orders. Fonseca, he said, don't be too heavy-handed, I don't want problems, just give him a little lesson and find out you know what, and as for you, Lima, behave yourself, I spotted that blackjack tucked inside your shirt, but no head blows, mind, what I want is a ribs and kidney job, where it hurts but doesn't leave marks. Just as you say, Captain, grunted the two thugs. They went through and shut the door behind them. Well then Dr. Pereira, said the seedy runt, we'll just have a little chat while my assistants get on with their work. I want to call the police, insisted Pereira. The police? smiled the seedy runt, but I am the police, Dr. Pereira, or at least I'm standing in for them, because at night even our policemen have to sleep, you know, our police protect us all the livelong day but at night they go to beddy-bye because they're asleep on their feet, what with all the criminals there are around, people like your guest here who've lost their sense of patriotism, but tell me, Dr. Pereira, what made you get yourself into this mess? I haven't gotten myself into any mess, retorted Pereira, I simply engaged an assistant for the *Lisboa*. Of course, Dr. Pereira, of course, said the seedy runt, but you really ought to have made inquiries beforehand, you should've consulted the police or your boss and given them the particulars of your so-called assistant, do you mind if I help myself to a cherry?

Pereira maintains that at this point he got up from his chair. He had sat down because his heart was racing, but now he got up and said: Those were cries, I tell you! I want to see what's going on in my bedroom. The seedy runt jerked up his pistol. I wouldn't do that if I were you, Dr. Pereira, he said, my men have a delicate job to do and you wouldn't find it pleasant to watch, you're a sensitive man Dr. Pereira, an intellectual, and what's more your heart's not strong, there are sights that just aren't good for you. I want to call my editor-in-chief, persisted Pereira, let me call my editor-in-chief. The seedy runt gave him a sarcastic leer. Your editor-in-chief is fast asleep by this time, he replied, very likely in the arms of a beautiful woman, you know, your editor-in-chief is a real man, Dr. Pereira, he's got balls, not like you who go looking for young blondies with pretty assholes. Pereira took a step forward and slapped the man's face. The stunted weed struck him a sharp blow with the pistol, and blood started dribbling from Pereira's mouth. You shouldn't have done that, Dr. Pereira, said the stunted weed, they told me to treat you with respect but there's a limit to everything, it's not my fault if you're such an imbecile as to hide traitors in your home, I could easily put a bullet through your windpipe and I'd do it with pleasure, the only reason I don't is that they've told me to treat you with respect, but don't take advantage, Dr. Pereira, don't take advantage or I might forget myself.

Pereira maintains that at this point he heard another strangled cry and that he hurled himself towards the door. But the stunted weed got there first and shoved him back. For all his bulk this shove sent Pereira reeling. Listen to me Dr. Pereira, said the seedy runt, don't force me to use my gun, it'd be a real pleasure to put a bullet through your windpipe or maybe your heart, which is your weak spot, but I'm not going to because we don't want any corpses, we've only come to give a little lesson in patriotism, and you could do with a spot of patriotism yourself come to that, seeing as in your paper you never publish anything but Frog writers. Pereira sat down again, he maintains, and said: It's only the French writers who've shown any guts in times like these. Allow me to inform you that Frog writers are a load of shit, said the seedy runt, they should all be put against the wall and shot and then pissed on. You're a vulgar lout, said Pereira. Vulgar but patriotic, replied the seedy runt, I'm not like you, Dr. Pereira, I don't exploit Frog writers to vent my antipatriotic sentiments.

At that moment the door flew open. The two thugs came out. They seemed breathless and nervous. The kid didn't want to talk, they said, so we gave him a lesson, we had to get tough and maybe we'd better scram. Did you go too far? asked the seedy runt. Don't know, replied the one called Fonseca, but we'd better take off. And he sprang for the door, his companion at his heels. Listen Dr. Pereira, said the seedy runt, you haven't seen us here, don't try to get smart, forget all about your new pals, just bear in mind that this was a friendly visit, because next time we come it might well be for you, have you got the message? Pereira locked the door behind them and listened until their footsteps faded away, he maintains. Then he rushed to the bedroom and found Monteiro Rossi sprawled on the carpet. Pereira gave him a gentle tap-tap on the cheek and said: Monteiro Rossi, try and pull yourself together, it's all over. But Monteiro Rossi didn't budge. So Pereira went to the bathroom, soaked a towel and wiped the boy's face with it. Monteiro Rossi, he repeated, it's all over, they've gone away, wake up. Only then did he realize that the towel had come away all red with blood, Monteiro Rossi's hair was sodden with it, his eyes were wide open and staring at the ceiling. Pereira slapped his cheek again, but Monteiro Rossi gave no sign of coming to. Pereira grabbed his wrist, felt his pulse. But life had ceased to flow in Monteiro Rossi's veins. Then Pereira closed those staring blue eyes and covered the face with the towel. He stretched out the legs, he didn't wish to leave him all huddled up like that, he maintains, so he stretched his legs out straight, as was only right for the legs of a dead man. And his next thought was that he had to act quickly, very quickly indeed, for time was short, Pereira maintains.

# TWENTY-FIVE

Pereira maintains that a wild idea had struck him, but he thought that maybe he could pull it off. He put on his jacket and left the building. Opposite the Cathedral was a late-night café with a public telephone. Pereira entered and gave the place a quick glance. There were a few night birds playing cards with the proprietor. The waiter was a sleepy youth lounging behind the counter. Pereira ordered a lemonade, then made his way to the telephone and dialed the number of the thalassotherapeutic clinic in Parede. He asked to speak to Dr. Cardoso. Dr. Cardoso has already retired to his room, who is calling please? said the voice of the switchboard operator. This is Dr. Pereira, said Pereira, the matter is urgent. I'll go and call him, if you don't mind waiting, said the voice, it will take him a minute or two to get down. Pereira waited patiently until Dr. Cardoso came on the line. Good evening Dr. Cardoso, there's something important I have to tell you, but I can't do so just now. What is it, Dr. Pereira, asked Dr. Cardoso, don't you feel well? As a matter of fact I don't, replied Pereira, but that's not the point, the fact is that a very serious problem has arisen at home, I'm not sure if my private phone is under surveillance, but that doesn't matter just now, I can't say more for the moment but I need your help, Dr. Cardoso. Tell me how I can help, said Dr. Cardoso. Well, Dr. Cardoso, said Pereira, tomorrow at midday I'm going to call you and ask you this favor, to pretend to be a bigwig in the censorship office and say that my article has been given the go-ahead, that's all. I don't see what you're driving at, said Dr. Cardoso. Listen Dr. Cardoso, said Pereira, I'm calling you from a café and I can't go into details, at home I have a problem such as you can't even imagine, but you'll learn about it in the evening edition of the *Lisboa*, it'll be down there in black and white, but you've got to do me this big favor, you must state that my article has your consent, you understand? I want you to say that the Portuguese police are not afraid of scandals, that it's a clean police force and has no fear of scandals. I get your message, said Dr. Cardoso, I'll be waiting for your call at midday.

The moment he got home Pereira went into the bedroom and removed the towel from Monteiro Rossi's face. He covered him with a sheet. Then he went back next door and sat down at his typewriter. He wrote a title, "Journalist Assassinated," then double-spaced and started to type: "His name was Francesco Monteiro Rossi, his father was Italian. He contributed articles and obituaries to this newspaper. He wrote texts on many great writers of our time, including Mayakovsky, Marinetti, D'Annunzio, Lorca. His articles have not yet been published, but perhaps one day they will be. He was a spirited young man who loved life, and instead it fell to his lot to write about death. A task he never shirked. But last night death sought him out. While he was dining with the editor of the culture page of the *Lisboa*, Dr. Pereira, the writer of this article, three armed men forced their way into the apartment. They stated that they were Political Police, but produced no documents to support their claim. It is almost unthinkable that they were official police officers, because they wore civilian clothes, and moreover it is to be hoped that the police in this country do not employ such methods. My conviction is that they were gangsters acting with the complicity of persons in high places, and the authorities would do well to inquire into this ugly business. Their leader was a skinny little person with a mustache and a small goatee. The other two addressed him as Captain, and he several times called them by name. These names, unless fictitious, are Fonseca and Lima. They are both tall, powerful men of swarthy complexion and apparently low intelligence. While the skinny man kept the writer of this article covered with a pistol, Fonseca and Lima dragged Monteiro Rossi into the bedroom to carry out what they called an interrogation. The present writer heard blows and smothered cries. Then the two men returned and said their work was done. The three of them hurriedly left the present writer's home, threatening him with death if he disclosed the occurrence. The present writer hastened to the bedroom but could do no more than ascertain the decease of young Monteiro Rossi. He had been beaten to a pulp, and the blows, inflicted with a blackjack or the butt of a pistol, had smashed his skull. His corpse is to be found on the second floor of number twenty-two, Rua da Saudade, the residence of the present writer. Monteiro Rossi was an orphan and had no relatives. He was in love with a beautiful sweet girl whose name is unknown to us. We only know that she had copper-colored hair and loved literature. To this girl, should she read this, we offer our sincerest condolences and deepest affection. We urge the competent authorities to maintain careful vigilance over these episodes of violence which under their wing, and perhaps with the direct complicity of certain persons in high places, are today being perpetrated here in Portugal."

Pereira double-spaced again and then, beneath and to the right, he typed his name: PEREIRA. He signed it simply Pereira because that was the way everyone knew him, by his surname, that was how he had signed all his crime reports for so many years and a day.

He raised his eyes to the window and saw that dawn was breaking over the fronds of the palm trees of the barracks across the way. He heard a bugle call. Pereira sank back into an armchair and nodded off. When he awoke it was already broad daylight and he took a startled look at the clock, he maintains. He had to be quick off the mark. He shaved, rinsed his face in cold water and left the flat. He found a taxi in front of the cathedral and gave his office address. There he found Celeste in her cubbyhole. She greeted him fulsomely. Nothing for me? asked Pereira. Nothing new, Dr. Pereira, replied Celeste, except they've given me a week off. And waving the calendar at him she continued: I'll be back next Saturday, for a whole week you'll have to do without me, nowadays the State protects the underprivileged, people like me I mean, we're not organized into corporations for nothing. We'll try to bear your absence as best we may, muttered Pereira, as he plodded upstairs. He entered the office, took the "Obituaries" file from the shelf, put it in a leather briefcase and left again. He called in at the Café Orquídea, reckoning that he had time to sit down for five minutes and have a drink. He settled himself at a table. Dr. Pereira, a lemonade? asked Manuel brightly. No thanks, replied Pereira, I'll have a dry port, I'd rather have a dry port. This is something really exceptional, Dr. Pereira, said Manuel, and at this time of day too, but I'm pleased because it means you're on the mend. Manuel gave him a glass and left the bottle on the table. Look Dr. Pereira, he said, I'll leave the bottle, so if you want another glass just help yourself, and if you'd like a cigar I'll bring you one right away. Yes, thank you, bring me a mild cigar, said Pereira, but incidentally Manuel, what about your friend who gets the BBC, what's the news? It seems the republicans are getting clobbered, said Manuel, but you know Dr. Pereira, he added lowering his voice, they also said something about Portugal. Did they now, said Pereira, and what did they say about us? They said we're living under a dictatorship, replied the waiter, and that the police are torturing people. And what do you have to say about that, Manuel? asked Pereira. Well what do you say, Dr. Pereira? he replied, scratching his head, you're a journalist, you're in the know. I say that the English are perfectly right, said Pereira. He lit his cigar, paid the bill, went out and took a taxi to the printer's. When he got there he found the foreman all huffing and puffing.

We're going to press in exactly an hour, said the foreman, you did a good thing Dr. Pereira, putting in that story by Camilo Castelo Branco, it's a beaut, I read it as a schoolboy but it's still a beaut. We'll have to cut it by a column, said Pereira, I've got a piece here for the end of the culture page, it's an obituary. Pereira handed him the sheet of paper, the foreman read it through and scratched his head. Dr. Pereira, said the foreman, this is pretty tricky, you bring me this at the last moment and it's not passed by censor, seems to me that this is no joke. Look here Senhor Pedro, said Pereira, we've known each other for nearly thirty years, ever since I started crime reporting for the best paper in Lisbon, and have I ever gotten you into trouble? Never, replied the foreman, but times have changed, it's not like it was in the old days, now there's all this bureaucracy and I have to toe the line, Dr. Pereira. Senhor Pedro, said Pereira, the censor's office gave me permission by word of mouth, I called them from my office half an hour ago, I spoke to Major Lourenço, he gave me the all clear. All the same it'd be better to ring the Chief, objected the foreman. Pereira heaved a deep sigh and said: Very well, Senhor Pedro, call him then. The foreman dialed the number and Pereira listened. And his heart was in his mouth. He realized that the foreman was speaking to Senhora Filipa. Then the foreman replaced the receiver and said: The Chief's out to lunch, I spoke to his secretary and he won't be back until three o'clock. The paper's already off the press by three, said Pereira, we can't wait until then. You're telling me, said the foreman, I don't know what to do, Dr. Pereira. Look here, suggested Pereira, the best thing would be to call the censor's office direct, maybe we can talk to Major Lourenço. Major Lourenço! exclaimed the foreman as if the very name struck panic into him, talk direct to Major Lourenço? He's a friend of mine, said Pereira as nonchalantly as he could, I read him my article just now, he's perfectly amenable, I'm in contact with him every day, Senhor

Pedro, it's part of my job. Pereira took over the telephone and dialed the number of the thalassotherapeutic clinic at Parede. At the other end came Dr. Cardoso's voice. Good afternoon Major, said Pereira, this is Dr. Pereira of the *Lisboa*, I'm here at the printer's with a view to inserting the article I read you this morning but the foreman here is worried because it hasn't got your clearance stamp, do please see if you can reassure him, I'll pass him to you. He gave the foreman the receiver and watched every flicker of an eyelid. Senhor Pedro began to nod. Certainly Major, he said, very good Major. Then he hung up and looked at Pereira. Well? asked Pereira. He says the Portuguese police are not afraid of scandal, replied the printer, that there are a lot of criminals around who must be denounced and that your article absolutely has to appear today, Dr. Pereira, that's what he said. And the foreman added: He also said tell Dr. Pereira to write an article about the soul, because that's something we all need, that's exactly what he said, Dr. Pereira. Just his little joke, said Pereira, however tomorrow I'll be talking to him myself.

He left the article with Senhor Pedro and made it to the door. He felt like a wet rag and his insides were churning madly. It occurred to him to stop for a sandwich at the café at the corner, but in the end he only ordered a lemonade. Then he took a taxi as far as the cathedral. He entered the flat warily, afraid that someone might be lying in wait for him. But there was no one there, only an enormous silence. He went into the bedroom and gazed a moment at the sheet that covered Monteiro Rossi. Then he fetched a small suitcase, packed the absolute minimum and the file of obituaries, went to the bookshelves and began to hunt through Monteiro Rossi's passports. Eventually he came across one that suited him. It was a French passport, a good piece of work, the photograph was of a fat man with bags under his eyes, and the age was about right. His name was Baudin, François Baudin. It sounded like a pretty good name to Pereira. He slipped the passport into the suitcase and picked up the picture of his wife. I'm taking you with me, he told it, you'd much better come with me. He packed it face up, so that she could breathe freely. Then he took a look around and glanced at his watch.

Better be getting along, the *Lisboa* would be out any moment and there was no time to lose, Pereira maintains.